HE SPUN THE PLATTER
TO THE TUNE OF DEATH—

*Layton ran out into the corridor. He strode over to
the dressing room numbered two and yanked the
door open. The room was empty.*

He darted across the corridor to the opposite
dressing room, intending to work his way from
room to room all the way down the hall. It was
not necessary. He found Tutter King in dressing
room one.

The disc jockey was on the floor, sprawled on his
back, legs wide, mouth and eyes open. The handle
of what appeared to be an ice pick protruded from
the left side of his chest. Kneeling, Layton felt for
a pulse. King was dead!

More Suspense from SIGNET

Death
Spins the Platter

ELLERY QUEEN

A SIGNET BOOK

NEW AMERICAN LIBRARY

TIMES MIRROR

Published by arrangement with
Manfred B. Lee and Frederic Dannay

SIGNET, SIGNET CLASSICS, MENTOR, PLUME AND MERIDIAN BOOKS
are published by The New American Library, Inc.,
1301 Avenue of the Americas, New York, New York 10019

FIRST SIGNET PRINTING, JUNE, 1973

3 4 5 6 7 8 9 10 11

LIST OF PRINCIPALS

IN

"THE KING'S FINAL SHOW"

« 1 »

Layton engineered his lanky frame from behind the wheel of his battered six-year-old coupe. He had parked in the middle of a long line of racy little foreign cars, most of them convertibles, and he half-expected some flunky to come rushing out of the building and order him to get his proletarian heap the hell off the premises.

The fantasy in white stucco that housed the TV station was only one story high, but it monopolized an entire block along Sunset Boulevard. The entrance from the parking lot brought him into the reception room of a dream world. It was presided over by a glittery blonde who looked as if she had stepped out of a time machine from the year 8162.

The futuristic blonde looked him over in a crystalline sort of way, and he said, "I'm Jim Layton of the *Los Angeles Bulletin*."

"Oh, yes," she said, thawing. "You're covering The King's Session final show. But it doesn't start for over an hour."

"I thought I'd interview the two principals beforehand."

"Whatever you'd like," the receptionist said. Whatever? Layton thought. She looked good enough to eat. "Mr. Hathaway said you're to have the run of the station. Would you like to talk to Mr. King first?"

"Is he here?"

"I think he's in his dressing room. Number 2." She pointed a long platinum-colored fingernail toward a corridor to the left. "Go past those offices and turn right at the end of the hall. Or . . ." Swiveling in her chair, she indicated another hallway. Everything swiveled with her. "This one takes you around to the main entrance to Studio A, where King's Session is telecast. You might like to see it before you talk to Mr. King. If you'll go on through Studio A and out the opposite door, you'll find yourself at the same turn in the hall as if you went the other way." She smiled at him. "Get it?"

"I'd sure like to," Layton said regretfully, "but, baby, I'm working." He decided on the official studio route.

The door marked *Studio A* opened into a big functional room with a naked floor. Spotted about were three unmanned TV cameras, three overhead microphone booms, and, off to one side, a record turntable. The King's Session

7

had the 3-P.M. time slot and it was only ten of two, but already about fifty teenagers of both sexes were clustered like grapes around the dance floor, and others were lying all over the folding-type chairs lining the walls.

As Layton moved past one of the clusters he heard a boy say, "After he opens the show, at my signal everybody start clapping and whistling and yelling and don't stop, and I mean don't. Let'em all know what we think of this crummy deal."

Layton paused curiously. The boy was thin and serious-faced, wearing horn-rimmed eyeglasses with thick lenses. He was about seventeen. This might be as good a time as any to get a typical Tutter King fan's viewpoint about the disc jockey's troubles.

Edging into the group, he said to the boy, "I'm from the *Bulletin*. If I get your pitch, you're organizing a claque for King—"

"A what?" the boy said.

"Well, it's a kind of rooting section, only it gets paid."

A rather ominous quiet fell. The bespectacled boy said, "You mean, mister, you think Tutter King's paying us—or me—to whip up a storm today?"

"Is he?" Layton asked.

"No," the boy said. He turned away.

"Wait a minute, kid," Layton said. "No hard feelings. If it's not for dough, then why are you doing it?"

The boy turned back. "To show the viewers and the brass of this station we're still behind Tut a hundred per cent." They were all around Layton now, making multiple sounds of approval. Absurdly, he began to feel uneasy.

"You don't think King should have been fired?"

A plain-looking girl, no more than sixteen, thrust her plump face toward Layton. "Tutter's done more for us kids than anybody on television. They're always yacking about juvenile delinquency, but when a good, clean program like the King's Session comes along, they kill it!"

"You think the station had any choice?" Layton asked. "In the face of public opinion?"

"They were probably pressured into it," the boy with the glasses admitted. "But the public's all wet. What did Tut King do that was so bad?"

Layton said dryly, "He admitted to a congressional investigating committee that he'd accepted more than a hundred thousand dollars a year under the table to plug second- and third-rate records, that's all." He took a notebook out of his pocket. "Mind giving me your names?"

"I don't mind one darn bit," the boy said. "I'm Wayne

Mission, and I'm president of the L. A. Tutter King Fan Club. And you can quote anything I say."

"Me, too," the plump girl said. "Nora Perkins. I'm vice president."

Others in the group volunteered their names, and Layton dutifully wrote them all down. He turned back to the boy with the glasses. "Wayne, don't you think Tutter King was morally wrong in accepting payola to plug inferior records?"

"Morally, shmorally," the boy retorted. "He paid his taxes, didn't he? Who isn't on the take these days? Cops organizing burglary rings. Politicians on big lobbyists' pay rolls. Labor leaders robbing union tills and selling out their own members. Industry in price-fixing conspiracies, doing phony advertising, mislabeling. And all those great big marvelous TV giveaway shows a while back—all fixed. Payola's everywhere, mister. So why all this jazz about Tutter King plugging some records for a fee? Who'd he hurt?"

"You," Layton said.

"Me?" Young Mission was astonished.

"Aren't you sore, having bad music crammed into your ears just to line a disc jockey's pockets?"

"Aaah, you squares all act as though Tutter'd violated a sacred trust or something. What's the difference what records we go for? It's the beat we dig, anyway. You'd think Tutter'd been selling us dope."

One of the other boys said mockingly, "Yeah!" and they all laughed.

The kid's got a point, Layton thought. Maybe in a morally anesthetized society the only sin *was* to be caught.

They're all out of step but me, he thought.

"What's your opinion, Nora?" he asked the girl.

"Tutter's the dreamiest," she replied. "I wouldn't care if he'd robbed the Bank of America."

"Thanks, both of you." If nice kids like these thought that way, what hope was there?

The reporter shook his head and drifted toward the other studio door, the one lettered *Studio Employees Only*. He pushed through and found himself at the joint of an L-shaped corridor. At the end of the branch to his right he could make out the fluid glitter of the receptionist. Straight ahead, dressing rooms lined both sides of the L's other arm. At the far end of this hall gleamed the glass of a control booth to another studio.

The door of the dressing room labeled 2 was open.

Layton was about to negotiate the few yards between him and the open dressing room when the sound of a bolt being turned over made him look to his left. As he turned,

9

a door opened noisily; in the silence of the corridors it was startling. A perky little redhead, all curves, was just coming out of a room adjoining Studio A, adjusting her blouse. She frowned when she saw Layton, walked quickly past him, and went into dressing room 2.

Curious, Layton strolled over to the room she had just vacated. The door had remained open, and he looked in. He grinned. It was a tiny room, windowless, with a wash-bowl and an unscreened toilet; on the door, he now saw, was the legend *Ladies—Employees Only*. No wonder the redhead had frowned!

In her embarrassment at being caught still adjusting her clothing she had forgotten to shut the door. Layton pulled it to; its self-closing device was out of order.

He drifted over to room 2, wondering who the redhead was. She had looked familiar.

The curvy redhead was seated at a small table across from a man; between them lay two containers of black coffee, apparently cold. Her hand cupped the man's chin across the table and she was leaning far forward, smiling, her rather thin lips a tantalizing two inches from his.

They became aware of Layton in the doorway simultaneously. The woman sat back, annoyed. The man turned his head to give Layton an inquiring look. He was slim, on the Ivy League side, with a smooth, clean, open face that just missed being handsome. Close up, in the flesh, he seemed even younger than the thirty-five years he publicly admitted to. He reminded Layton of a jockey—the horse variety, ageless.

"Mr. King? I'm Jim Layton of the *Bulletin*. Spare me a few minutes?"

"Well, hello, Jim." The disc jockey rose and shook Layton's hand warmly, his features slipping by long practice into the charming and boyish smile that was his public expression number one. "Sure enough. Hathaway sent me a memo you'd be here with the rest of the mourners. Oh! Lola Arkwright, my assistant."

"Hello, Miss Arkwright," Layton said.

"Hello," she said. She was furious.

Layton was amused. According to his publicity, Tutter King was an incorrigible bachelor without a libido in his make-up—a sort of two-dimensional man, an image on a screen, exuding sex but with the untouchability of a monk. It was his principal appeal to the teenage girls; there was no more danger in him than in a dream. It was no accident that Nora Perkins had called him "the dreamiest."

Layton doubted that Lola Arkwright thought of King

that way. He remembered her now. She was the girl on The King's Session who operated the turntable.

"Here, sit down, Jim," King said, holding out the chair he had been occupying. The only other seat in the dressing room was covered by the redhead's full little bottom. "How about some coffee? There's a coin-operated machine down the hall. Lola, go get Mr. Layton some like a doll."

"For you I'll do anything, darling," the redhead said. "But on your dime, not mine."

"I don't care for any, thanks just the same," Layton said. He remained standing, and so did King. "Mr. King, how do you feel about having your show canceled? Think KZZX was justified in firing you?"

"Call me Tutter, or Tut," the disc jockey said with a smile. "I don't go for this formal stuff."

"Okay, Tut. Do you think you got a raw deal, or don't you?"

King's smile faded effortlessly into an expression of frank gravity. "What do you think, Jim?"

"Reporters aren't supposed to have opinions. It's yours I'm paid to get."

King sat down at the table and reached for one of the coffee containers. "Nobody's even suggested that I did anything illegal. I'm not under indictment for any crime. There's no law against accepting fees to plug records. And every cent I've ever received I've reported on my tax returns."

"My paper knows the legality of your position," Layton said. "What I'm here for is your opinion of the ethics involved."

King drained the cup of its cold contents.

"I'll give you *my* opinion," Lola said acidly. "I think this whole deal stinks. Tutter's one of the finest guys I've ever known."

"Shut up, doll," King said. "Well, Jim, I'll match my ethics against the next fellow's. I gave the record companies what they paid for, and I can't see that I damaged a darn soul in the process."

"Then it's your position that there's nothing wrong in accepting payola in return for popularizing songs you know to be dogs?"

King's slight shoulders shrugged boyishly. "Most pop tunes today are pretty bad, Jim. If I only spun the platters I really go for, I couldn't run The King's Session for a week."

Layton wrote the answer down in his notebook. The slightest vertical line appeared between King's eyes. He said suddenly, "How old are you, Jim?"

11

"Thirty-four." Layton was surprised.

"Then you must remember—when we were kids—how people flipped over 'Flat-foot Floogie,' 'Mairsie Doats,' and all the rest of them. They were a lot worse than some of these rock-'n'-roll lyrics."

"I'd appreciate a direct statement, Mr. King."

"Tutter," King said, smiling again.

"Tutter. Do you or don't you think that what you did was wrong?"

"I didn't do anything anyone else wouldn't have done in my place."

"That still isn't answering the question."

"Suppose you'd been running The King's Session. Would you have turned down a hundred G's a year for slanting your plugs?"

"All right, you've sucked me in." Layton grinned. "You want my answer? Yes, if I had to take it under the table."

The red-haired girl said softly, "That's why you're a two-bit reporter."

"I said shut up, Lola," King said just as softly. "I respect your views, Jim. But I honestly think my only offense was getting caught, and having the whole thing twisted to make it look as if I were a crook or something."

Layton wrote it down.

"As far as KZZX is concerned," the disc jockey went on, "they just folded under the heat. It took some folding, because The King's Session has been their biggest moneymaker. I'll tell you something else, Jim."

"Yes?" Layton looked up alertly.

"The whole story hasn't come out."

"What do you mean?"

"Let's just say some of those who've yelled loudest for my scalp could stand a little investigating themselves."

"You mean others were involved in the payola?"

King's smile this time was not charming. "You staying for the show?"

"Now I am," Layton said.

"Good, because I'm making an important statement just before I sign off."

"About these others being involved, or have you changed the subject?"

"Just stick around. Nice meeting you, Jim."

"Thanks," Layton said, putting away his notebook. He nodded to the redhead and turned to the doorway.

Lola said poutingly, "Now don't you print anything bad about my Tutter."

"Where do I find Hathaway's office?" Layton asked.

"Just around the corner, Jim. Second door to the right."

King was breathing down the redhead's neck as Layton left.

« 2 »

The firm-fleshed, ruddy, handsome man with the vigorous white hair who rose from his desk in the station manager's office to squeeze Layton's hand with unnecessary strength looked exactly like the former movie star he was.

George Hathaway had been one of the box-office gold mines of the silent screen. As in so many other cases, the advent of sound in films had ended his screen career. There was no power or profit in a romantic male star who, when he opened his mouth, sounded like a magnified mouse. As he liked to say, "I heard the handwriting on the wall." He had promptly gone into the administrative end of radio and, ultimately, of television.

Layton had never met him before. Studying Hathaway now, the shrewd eyes, the hearty manner, the effortless charm, the newspaperman realized why Hathaway had made the successful transition from performer to executive with such ease. He had simply transferred his personal magnetism from the screen to an office.

Layton declined a cigar, and Hathaway leaned back in his ducal swivel chair to regard his journalistic visitor with just the right blend of affability and concern.

"I hope my people have been cooperating, Mr. Layton?"

"No complaints," Layton said. "I've just had a talk with Tutter King."

"Sad case," Hathaway said, giving the shake of his head an appropriate sadness. "It's costing us a fortune to cancel The King's Session show. But of course we had no choice."

"You mean because of all those letters and calls from Outraged Parent?"

"Oh, it wasn't that alone," Hathaway said quickly. "We'd have had to let King go in any event."

"Why?"

"Why?" The executive seemed puzzled.

"Yes," Layton said. "If the public hadn't reacted as it did to his payola admission to the investigating committee, do you mean to say you'd have washed him out anyway?"

"Of course," Hathaway's sleek white brows drew together in a frown. "There are ethical standards in the television

13

industry, Mr. Layton. And certainly at KZZX. Tutter King had a special responsibility to keep his hands clean—all those teenagers, and so on. And if he doesn't feel that responsibility, KZZX does."

Layton took out his notebook. Hathaway eyed it with the slightest alarm.

"I mean," he went on rather hurriedly, "No one is shocked when a racketeer is convicted of income-tax evasion—quite the contrary, because his getting caught is a fine moral lesson for our youth—"

"I wonder," Layton murmured.

"I beg your pardon?"

Layton looked up. "Did I say it out loud? I was thinking that maybe convicting a notorious gangster for income-tax evasion doesn't constitute such a fine moral lesson for our youth, Mr. Hathaway. When it happens, haven't you ever asked yourself, Why wasn't he convicted of murder?"

Hathaway looked at him suspiciously. But only for a moment. He smiled, with a manly ruefulness "Perhaps I chose a poor example. I simply meant that teenagers identify themselves with their idols, and that's why their idols have to be like Caesar's wife."

"Caesar's wife." Layton wrote down. Then he looked up again. "It's been over a week, Mr. Hathaway, since King's testimony was made public by the congressional committee. Why has he been allowed on the air this week? Why wasn't the show killed at once?"

But the white-haired man was prepared for that. "Television programing is quite complex, Mr. Layton," he said smoothly. "You don't replace a two-hour, five-day-a-week show on a day's notice."

"You do if you're concerned about your performer's corrupting influence on youth."

Hathaway blew. His ruddy complexion turned mahogany, his fist came down on his desk, and the squeak of his voice mounted very nearly out of audible range. "Mr. Layton! You're not going to use that Mike Wallace technique on me! I don't have to stand for it, and I won't!"

"Just doing my job," Layton said. "All I asked was why King's show wasn't yanked right away."

"And I've told you! Programing takes *time*. We not only had to line up ten hours of replacement, we've had to sell King's sponsors on them!"

"Sponsors," Layton said, writing it down.

"Yes, *sponsors*—that dirty word! This is a business, Layton, not an ethical-culture society. I'm sick and tired of this —this Commie kind of attack whenever an honest industry

14

polices itself in its own protection! King pulled an inexcusable booboo—"

"And he's got to pay for it. I couldn't agree more." Layton put his notebook away and rose. "Thanks, Mr. Hathaway."

"Uh . . . one moment." The mahogany shade was fading to it normal rose, and Hathaway managed to overlay it with a normal smile. "There I go again. I'm afraid it's been a rough week for all of us—"

"Especially for Tutter King," Layton replied, returning the smile.

"Of course, of course. I feel simply dreadful about it. He's a fine fellow. Most unfortunate. But what can I do?" Hathaway spread his manicured hands in a man-to-man plea for understanding. "You can't know the pressures a man in my job has to cope with, Mr. Layton. But that's no excuse for losing my temper. I sincerely apologize."

"No apology necessary," Layton said cheerfully, glancing at his wristwatch.

"I don't want you thinking that self-interest was our only motive. I really meant what I said about our feeling of responsibility toward the youngsters—"

"I understand, Mr. Hathaway. Say, *I* don't want to miss that telecast. Thanks again."

"Don't mention it," George Hathaway said bitterly. He remained standing behind his magnificent desk long after Layton was gone.

As for Layton, he was recalling Tutter King's cryptic hint about others having been involved, and he was wondering just how good an actor George Hathaway had been. Unfortunately, Layton had been a small boy in Hathaway's heyday, and the Late Show never ran silents.

Studio A was boiling. King stood on the bandless bandstand with his charm showing, tolerating the man with the light meter. But he was an island in the storm. Lola Arkwright, the redhead, was feverishly sorting records at the turntable. The camera crews were busy making their final checks; one camera was aimed at King, one was preparing to shoot the dance floor, the third was apparently being made ready for special shots. The sound-engineer team was swarming about the microphones.

The fifty or so teenagers had quadrupled by now. They milled about, making beelike noises. Layton noticed Wayne Mission and Nora Perkins darting from group to group.

And something new had been added. A small group of adults sat on the folding chairs near the main door. Layton's eye was automatically attracted to the woman occupying the chair nearest the door.

She was slim and svelte, with masses of impeccably coifed black hair that reflected the studio lights. Her pallor was almost studied, as if she had been made up by Charles Addams. And that street dress she's wearing, Layton thought, cost somebody three hundred bucks.

But it was her face that fascinated him. There was a rigidity about it that reminded him of a department-store dummy. It had the same blank, remote expression, a sort of determined deadness, that stirred his reporter's curiosity. Layton's first thought was that she was asleep with her eyes open. Then he decided that it was caused by a shyness bordering on fear. And then he changed his mind; it was not shyness bordering on fear, it was fear itself.

Layton's speculations were shattered by the blow of a voice roaring for quiet.

"Thirty seconds."

All sounds ceased. Then a red light on the camera focused upon Tutter King suddenly glowed.

The smile of boyish charm lit up King's smooth, clean face on the split second of the red light's appearance.

"Afternoon once again, drakes and ducklin's, and welcome to The King's Session, presented each weekday at this same time by KZZX-TV, and brought to you by the fine products we'll mention from time to time during the next two hours."

The famous King smile began to dim as the frank, manly voice paused. "As most of you probably know," the disc jockey continued, letting the smile come up again bravely, "this is the final TV appearance of yours truly. I'd be worse than a fool, I'd be ungrateful, if I took any credit for the wonderful success of The King's Session during the past five years. For that you wonderful fans out there—you kids in the studio"—the dance-floor camera came on, panning slowly—"you wonderful kids—" at the stricken young faces, and then camera number 1 returned Tutter King's image to the monitors—"are entirely responsible. Thank you. Thank you." His voice broke ever so little, and the silence in the studio suddenly became charged with tension.

But then Tutter King squared his shoulders and said in a strong voice, "But I don't intend to play any funeral marches today! We're going to have a *happy* time. Aren't we, colts and fillies?"

A vast *"YES"* rattled the microphones.

"You bet! Later in the program I want to introduce the various members of my staff, all the technicians, who've

16

worked so hard and anonymously to make these sessions so popular . . . and at the very end . . ."

Layton watched King's face closely. A nerve at the corner of the boyish mouth was making a tiny muscle quiver ever so slightly.

". . . and at the very end I'm going to make an important statement."

The smile that King was summoning back came, Layton thought, with uncharacteristic reluctance.

"But right now, cats and kittens, it's back to the old baton and . . . *Music, please!*"

He raised his arms, one hand poising a baton, and nodded to Lola Arkwright. But before the red-haired girl could apply the turntable arm to the record, the studio exploded.

The bespectacled president of the Tutter King Fan Club had done his work well. Applause, whistles, cheers, the high-pitched yells of the girls took over the air waves. Wayne Mission and Nora Perkins were standing dangerously on folding chairs, stage-managing the demonstration. One block of boys, at young Mission's further signal, began stamping on the dance floor in perfect unison. Above the pandemonium individual voices, hysterical with excitement, rose in screams of "We—want—Tutter, we—want—Tutter!" until, infecting the others, all other sounds turned into a vast chanted thunder: *"WE—WANT—TUTTER!"*

King's lips were moving, but his voice was drowned in the tidal wave of noise. He tried to quiet them with gestures, half-smiling, half-serious. But they paid no attention to him; and finally he dropped his arms and shrugged helplessly into the camera.

Layton turned his own camera eye on the Studio A control room. It was the scene of a fierce argument in pantomime, obviously over whether to cut the program off the air. He saw the director snatch a telephone, listen, then nod, cut the connection, and sit back in resignation. The station brass—Layton wondered whether it was Hathaway himself —had decided to ride out the storm rather than risk studio devastation.

King began gesturing again, pleading into his microphone. Gradually his voice became audible, "Kids . . . kids . . . kids . . ." and then, as suddenly as it had begun, the noise stopped. Layton saw Wayne Mission step off his chair and sit down on it, folding his arms.

"Thank you," Tutter King said huskily, "thank you, geese and goslin's, for a demonstration of loyalty I'll remember all the rest of my life. If you were trying to break me up, you darn near succeeded!

"But time's a-wastin', as the fellow said," King continued

17

briskly, nodding to the control room, "so—on with the dance! But first," he went on, reading the teleprompter, "here's an important message from Plush, the Soap That's in Love with Your Skin. Ladies, are your hands red and unsightly from the strong detergents and bleaches in common household use today? Do you find yourself trying to hide them under the tablecloth when that Man in Your Life takes you out to that divine dining place you've so looked forward to? Then take my advice and listen to this suggestion."

The red light on camera 1 blinked out and a commercial film took Tutter King's place on the monitor screens. Layton kept watching the teenagers. They were paying no attention to the commercial. They simply stood and sat around, suspended in time, waiting for something he was unable to fathom. And King . . . King was waiting with them. Then the commercial went off, and camera 1's light went on again, and King raised his baton again, and Lola Arkwright spun the first platter, and the dancing began.

It was a long, deadly session for Jim Layton; he had never been so bored in his life. King's patter in introducing the records seemed to him cliché ridden, unbright, and unfunny; the red-haired girl tended the turntable like an automaton; the dance-floor camera kept recording the activity on the floor, such as it was. The dancing had a stylized lifelessness, the dancers a lack of facial expression, that reminded Layton of a congress of zombies, with Tutter King as the mad scientist. Sometimes King sauntered on to the floor with a portable microphone to chat with this zombie couple or that; sometimes he introduced a commercial; occasionally the perky redhead joined him in both conversations and commercials.

The prevailing dullness was too much for some of the adults near the door; after the first quarter-hour three of them rose and left. The well-dressed woman with the glossy black hair was not one of them. She scarcely moved during the entire first hour; her slender gloved hands remained quiescent in her lap; she simply kept sitting there, rigid. Layton, keeping out of camera range, maneuvered himself around the studio for a closer look at her. He had judged her from across the studio to be in her mid-twenties. He now saw that she was at least thirty, perhaps older.

At the four-o'clock station break there was a ten-minute interlude for a newscast. King reminded his viewers with a cheery smile to stay tuned for the second portion of his show and the "surprise announcement" he had promised before his sign off; the red light on his camera vanished; Studio A went off the air; the teenagers immediately broke

18

into animated conversation, laughing and horsing around, as if the blinding of the cameras' eyes had lifted the spell that had bewitched them; and Tutter King with utter self-effacement slipped like a thin shadow through the door marked *Studio Employees Only,* and disappeared.

Lola Arkwright slipped out directly after King.

The woman with the black hair stirred. She hesitated for perhaps fifteen seconds. Then, without warning, she jumped to her feet, ran to the door, opened it swiftly, and disappeared also. Layton could not have been more startled if she had suddenly yelled, "Allay-oop!" and done a handstand on the back of her chair.

By the time he was able to push through the densely clustered groups chattering on the dance floor and follow her into the corridor, she was gone.

Not only was there no sign of her in either arm of the L-shaped hall, but the disc jockey and his girl Friday had vanished, too.

« **3** »

Layton walked down the arm of the L that went past the dressing rooms. At the door to number 2 he hesitated. King and the redhead were probably in there; the door was closed this time and he had no excuse for opening it. But where had the scared brunette holed up? He peered into every dressing room along the corridor whose door was open, but they were all unoccupied.

She was probably in a hurry to get to the women's john, Layton thought with a grin, and what she'd been afraid of was that she wouldn't make it.

He backtracked and strolled down the other corridor. As he was passing the station manager's office a tall, trim, gray-haired man stepped out. He favored the reporter with the sort of vague, half-smiling nod politicians bestow on passers-by who might conceivably have once been introduced to them. The tall gray man strode up the corridor and around the corner, from where Layton had just come.

The man had not closed Hathaway's door, and Layton looked in. The outer office was unoccupied except for Hathaway's secretary, a thin, harried-looking female whose gray hair had recently had a blue rinse.

"Mr. Hathaway isn't here, Mr. Layton," she said. "You'll

19

find him in the Studio B and C control room. That's over beyond the dressing rooms."

"I've already had the pleasure remember?" Layton smiled. To his surprise, she smiled back. "I'm killing time till the King show goes back on. By the way, who was that man of distinction—the gent who just left?"

"Mr. Stander, Hubert Stander. He's chairman of the board."

"Looking for Hathaway?"

"Now, Mr. Layton," the secretary said, still smiling. "Come in and sit down, why don't you? In your job you probably walk your feet off."

"Thanks." Layton drifted in and dropped into a chair near her desk. "Cigarette?"

"That's not my vice," she said. Her voice was quite warm now. "But you go ahead and be as vicious as you want." She pushed an ash tray toward him.

"If you don't smoke, why do you have an ash tray on your desk?"

"So that people like you won't get ashes all over the floor, Mr. Layton."

Layton grinned. "Didn't I hear Hathaway call you Hazel?"

She nodded. "Hazel Grant."

"What do you think of Tutter King's being fired, Miss Grant?"

"Mrs. Grant."

"Sorry. Mrs. Grant."

"You mean for publication?"

"Any way you want."

"I would have to be off the record," she said, leaning back. "Mr. Hathaway would have forty kinds of fits if his secretary talked to the papers. Especially about this. The station's already given out its official statement."

"I know," Layton said. "Dripping with devotion to the public interest. But on account of I'm such a doll, Mrs. Grant—how *do* you feel about it?"

The woman stared at him quite steadily. "You promise not to mention my name?"

"I won't mention your name."

Hazel Grant glanced toward the open doorway. Then she said in a very low voice, "They've known for years about Tutter's arrangement with the record companies."

"Oh?" Layton said. "Who's they?"

"The station brass."

"Hathaway?"

She began to look nervous. "I don't know why I said anything at all. I really shouldn't have."

20

"Don't worry about it. Hathaway's known all along, huh?"

"Yes," she said with venom. "He's actually made envious remarks to me about the piles of money Tutter's been making under cover. He had to ignore what was going on because the program was so successful. Now that the story's come out, they all act surprised and self-righteous. I can't stand hypocrisy."

"I know what you mean," Layton said sympathetically. "By the way, was Tutter the only one in on it?"

"What?" Hazel Grant looked puzzled. "How do you mean?"

"Haven't you heard the story going around?"

"What story?"

"Why, I heard it myself just this afternoon in the station. That Tutter King had to split the payola with some of the big shots around here."

The woman's harassed eyes turned wary. "I hadn't heard anything like that."

"Then it isn't true?"

"I wouldn't know, Mr. Layton." She swung back to her typewriter, "I'm afraid I'll have to get to work."

Layton glanced at his watch. "And I'd better get to Studio A." He stubbed his cigarette out in the ash tray. "Enjoyed our chat, Mrs. Grant. Seeing you."

"Please." She was quite pale. "You won't quote me, will you? You promised."

"I keep my promises," Layton said. "Relax, Hazel."

He met no one on his way back to the studio. The big room was still noisy; the newscast had little more than a minute to run. The frightened-looking woman was again in her chair by the door, and she was still looking frightened. So much for my john theory, Layton thought. She was now the sole surviving adult in the studio audience.

He turned at hearing his name called. Lola Arkwright was running toward him. "Seen Tutter anywhere?" she panted.

"No. Wasn't he with you?"

"Would I be looking for him if he had been?" The girl was biting her lip. "I expected to find him back in the studio."

"Did you try his dressing room?"

"He wasn't there when I stopped by—"

"He wasn't?" Layton looked at her.

"Please, Mr. Layton! Will you do me a favor, quick?"

"Find him?"

"Yes! I'll have to stay here and fill in for him if he doesn't make air time." She glanced at the big studio clock.

21

It showed twenty-eight seconds to go. She hurried to the bandstand.

Layton ran out into the corridor. The hall lined with dressing rooms was deserted. In the other hall George Hathaway and Chairman of the Board Stander were just going into Hathaway's office.

Layton strode over to the dressing room numbered 2 and yanked the door open.

The room was empty.

He darted across the corridor to the opposite dressing room, the room numbered 1, intending to work his way from room to room all the way down the hall.

It was not necessary. He found Tutter King in dressing room 1.

The disc jockey was on the floor, sprawled on his back, legs wide, mouth and eyes open. The handle of what appeared to be an ice pick protruded from the left side of chest.

Kneeling, Layton felt for a pulse.

King was dead.

The newspaperman in him took control over his shocked faculties. King was dead, King was dead . . . but what about the room?

There was nothing about the room. It was a room, a dressing room. I'd make one hell of a detective, Layton thought.

He found himself in the corridor pulling the door to. Then he shook himself like a dog and made for Studio A.

It was back on the air. He eased the studio door open for a narrow look. The bandstand was unoccupied. Camera 1 was focused on the turntable. The redhead, coolly smiling, was talking into a microphone, a record in her hands. Good old Lola minding the store.

Wait till she takes inventory, Layton thought.

He made for Hathaway's office.

Hazel Grant looked up, startled, when he walked in. She half-rose from her typewriter.

"You can't go in there, Mr. Layton," she said quickly. "Mr. Hathaway is busy."

Layton paid no attention to her. He opened the door marked *Private* and let it bang against the wall. Behind him the blue-haired secretary was tugging at his jacket.

"Mr. Layton, I told you—"

"All right, Hazel," George Hathaway said in an annoyed voice. She retreated and Layton shut the door. The station manager was seated behind his desk and the man of distinction, Hubert Stander, was comfortably ensconced in the

22

chair Layton had occupied during his interview. "What is it, Layton? I'm in conference."

"That's good." Layton said, "because I've brought you something to confer about."

"What do you mean?"

"Tutter King is no more."

"What?" Hathaway looked perfectly blank.

"I just found him in dressing room 1 with what I think is an ice pick in his heart."

The two executives of KZZX got to their feet as one man. Hathaway half-turned to his right, then swung back to his left, as if he required reorientation for the route around his desk to the door. Stander was apparently a man of action as well as distinction; he was halfway across the outer office before Hathaway moved.

"And I wouldn't touch anything," Layton called after them. He turned to Mrs. Grant; she was back at her desk, staring after Hathaway and Stander.

"Is something wrong, Mr. Layton?"

"Get me the *Bulletin*," he said, "and when I'm finished put me through to police headquarters."

Her face went dead-white.

"I'll use Hathaway's phone."

He could hear her breathing on the extension throughout his report to the city desk. Layton shrugged. She got him the police captain in charge of the Homicide day watch, and this time she hung up. She was standing behind her desk with her hand to her mouth when he ran across the outer office.

Layton had just reached the joint of the L when the door of Studio A opened and Mystery Woman came out. He halted abruptly, and so did she.

"Pardon me." She had a voice that matched the hair, the clothes, and the fear. It was a glossy, expensive-sounding voice, and it was all tightened up with tension.

"Yes?" Layton said.

"I saw you in the studio." It was almost painful to listen to her. "Are you connected with the King show?"

"Why?"

"I thought you might know what's wrong."

"Is something wrong?" Layton said.

"It must be. Mr. King didn't come back after the intermission. That redheaded girl is doing it all by herself in there. Was he taken ill or something?"

Layton said, "You sound as if you have a personal interest."

To his surprise, her pale cheeks turned pink. He had forgotten that there were still women who blushed.

"Fan of his?"

"Well . . . sort of." He was even more surprised to see her eyes light up, her face turn lively and, in the process, the fear vanish. "I don't see any reason to keep it a secret any more," she said defiantly. "I'm Mrs. King."

"Mrs. King?" His echo of the name sounded stupid even to his ears. "You mean you're Tutter King's . . . ?"

"Tutter King's wife."

All Layton could think of to say was, "I thought Tut was a bachelor."

"We've been married ten years. Tutter felt it would hurt him with his fans, especially the girls, if they knew he had a wife. I've had to be *awfully* careful." Recalling the mask of fear she had been carrying around, Layton nodded. Maybe in private life, he thought, the charming Tutter King hadn't been so charming. "But it doesn't have to be that way any more. Not after today." With her face lighted up that way, she was almost beautiful. "Even Tutter said he'd have to go out of circulation till the talk died down. So now I can be Mrs. Tutter King right out loud."

"Yes, Mrs. King," Layton said. "Well . . ."

"But I don't know why I'm telling you all this," King's widow rattled on, "a perfect stranger!"

"It's probably my kind face," Layton muttered. And just then Hathaway and Stander came hurrying around the corner.

"Oh, Layton," Hathaway said. His ruddy cheeks had acquired a greenish tint. "He's dead, all right."

"Who's . . . dead?" the woman asked.

Quite mechanically Hathaway answered, "That damn fool King," and then he saw her really for the first time. "Who in God's name is this, Layton?"

"King's widow," Layton said; and he caught her just as her legs gave way.

Stander led the parade to the first door beyond the studio and unlocked it. Layton carried the woman in and Hathaway scuttled in behind him. The door said, *Chairman of the Board.* Stander closed it quickly.

The anteroom looked unused and smelled musty. There was no secretary. The tall gray man opened the inner door to a vast, awesome office with the same look and smell. The desk and board table were bare, the wastebasket empty. The room was dark; the Venetian blinds were closed.

"Better put her on the couch," the tall gray man said. He shut the inner door, too. "I'll get some water." Layton deposited the unconscious woman on a palace-sized tapestried couch that was unpleasantly moist to the touch. Stander

24

opened a lavatory door and went in and they heard water running.

"What is this, a tomb?" Layton grunted as he chafed the woman's hands. "Open a window, will you?"

Hathaway went over to a window, raised the blind a little, and began struggling. "It's only used four times a year," he mumbled. "For the quarterly board meetings." The window gave with a screech. "His widow," he said. "I'll be damned. How long were they married?"

"She said ten years."

"Here, let me," Hubert Stander said. He put his arm under her head and applied the edge of a water glass to her lips "Come on now, Mrs. King. Drink this." He said savagely, "Drink it!"

It slopped all over her chin and dripped onto her dress. She choked and opened her eyes and turned her face violently away.

"What are you trying to do, drown her?" Layton shoved the chairman of the board aside. "She'll be all right."

"I'll be all right," Mrs. Tutter King said; and then, almost apologetically, she put her hands to her face and began to cry.

Like the kid who's just been given the doll she's always wanted, Layton thought, only to have it kicked out of her hands and shatter on the floor.

They waited helplessly, turned away.

"Rough, rough," Hathaway said in a low voice, shaking his handsome head. "Who would ever have thought he'd take it this way?"

"Take what which way?" Layton said.

"Where have you been?" Chairman of the Board Stander said coldly. "The cancellation of the show, of course."

"But Mr. Hathaway just said—"

"Do you mean," the station manager said, staring at him, "you didn't realize . . ." Hathaway glanced over at the weeping widow and lowered his voice, "that Tutter committed suicide?"

"Suicide," Layton said. "Suicide?"

"Certainly!" Hubert Stander said.

"What else could it have been?" Hathaway said.

"Either you two are kidding," Layton said, "or this is a pretty bad dream."

Stander seemed to grow taller. "Hathaway tells me you're a newspaperman. I warn you, Layton—be very careful what you print! King was finished and he knew it. What's more, he knew he'd brought it all on his own head. He couldn't face the disgrace or the ruin of his career—"

"So he took the easy way out," Hathaway said excitedly.

25

Layton eyed them with total incredulity. "You mean like those old-time Spartans, or Romans, or whoever the hell they were—he drew his ice pick and fell on it?" The two executives reddened. "After announcing on the air that he'd make an important statement at the end of his show—but before he could make it?"

"The show," Hathaway muttered. "My God, the show." He seemed almost grateful for the opportunity Layton had given him to change the subject. "Lola—she's got to be told Tutter's not coming back—to finish the show herself—" He made for the door.

"Don't tell her why, George," Stander called after him. "We can't have her going to pieces on the air!" He smacked his forehead suddenly. "The police. We forgot to notify the police—"

"I didn't, Layton said.

The chairman of the board turned to glare at the press. "You wouldn't," he snarled and then he hurried after Hathaway.

« 4 »

The homicide team consisted of two sergeants who identified themselves as Harry Trimble and Ed Winterman. Trimble was an elongated bone of a man with close-cropped carrot hair and a diagonal scar that ran from his temple to his nose across his left eye, which was of glass. Winterman was broad and squat, with dark coloring and long arms. Trimble seemed to be Winterman's senior. Both looked very tough.

They had brought with them two police technicians and a photographer, who had gone to work immediately. The two detectives spent some time in dressing room 1 with the lab men. Then they rejoined the group waiting for them in Stander's office.

Sergeant Trimble's one working eye fixed on Layton. It seemed quite capable of doing double duty. "Aren't you Jim Layton of the *Bulletin?*"

The reporter nodded. "I kept stepping on your heels all through that Bentley homicide last year, Sergeant."

"A dilly." Trimble grinned. "And you sure kept me hopping. When you called in, Layton, you said you found King. How come?"

Layton explained the circumstances. Sergeant Trimble

listened in silence, fingering his glass eye as if he were worried it might pop out.

"Which one is George Hathaway?" Trimble asked when Layton had finished. He was consulting a piece of paper handed him by a uniformed man.

Hathaway said nervously, "I am."

"What's your story, Mr. Hathaway?"

"I have no story. I knew nothing about it until Layton ran into my office saying he'd just found Tutter King dead in dressing room 1. Mr. Stander—this gentleman here, the chairman of our board—was with me at the time, and we went immediately to dressing room 1—"

"Where we were extremely careful, Sergeant, not to touch anything," Hubert Stander said. "Although, of course, I can't vouch for Layton's not having touched anything when he found the body."

You elegant bastard, Layton thought admiringly.

"I'll vouch for it," Layton said.

"You sure?" the one-eyed detective asked him with the merest touch of a grin.

"Positive," Layton said gravely.

"You anything to add, Mr. Stander?"

"No."

Trimble turned to the black-haired woman, consulting the paper. She had used the lavatory off the board room to repair the damage to her make-up, and the Charles Addams pallor and expression were back on her face. There was a kind of resignation about her now, however, that had not been there before. As if she'd never had a real hope of release from her prison, anyway, Layton thought, and now she could slip right back into the old familiar nothing.

"You're Nancy King?" Sergeant Trimble said.

"Mrs. Tutter King." The voice, the nod, were quite lifeless.

Trimble's squat, swarthy partner opened his mouth for the first time. "My kid sister'll flip when she hears Tut King was married. She may not even go into mourning." Sergeant Winterman stared at King's widow as if he had a personal grievance.

"Cut it out, Ed," Trimble said. "What can you tell us about this, Mrs. King?

"Me?" She shrugged. "Not a thing."

"How about your husband's enemies? Maybe you can give us a lead."

"Come on, don't be bashful, Mrs. King," Winterman said. "This is an important case to the youth of America. Open up."

27

Nancy King shook her head. "If Tutter had any enemies, he never mentioned them to me."

Trimble glanced glumly at Layton. "This has all the makings of another dilly. Maybe sixty employees in the building, a couple of hundred studio guests—"

"I think you can rule most of them out for lack of opportunity, Trimble," Layton said. "The way this building's laid out ought to cut the suspects way down."

"Yeah?" the scarred detective said. "Tell me more."

"Wait—just—one—moment!" Stander and Hathaway had been exchanging furtive looks, and now the chairman of the board stepped forward. "Am I to understand, Sergeant Trimble, that you're going on the assumption this was *murder?*"

"What assumption would you go on, Mr. Stander?" Trimble asked in an interested voice.

"Why—anything but that! Why would anybody want to murder that unfortunate young fool? But he did have every reason to kill himself!"

"With an ice pick?" Sergeant Trimble asked.

"Oh, I don't know, Harry," his partner said. "They'll do it in some pretty screwy ways."

"You're absolutely right, Sergeant Winterman," George Hathaway said eagerly.

"That is," Winterman drawled, "if they're screwballs. But the way I always heard it, there wasn't a loose screw in King's noggin."

"We aren't ruling out suicide," Trimble said. "We aren't ruling out anything right now—including murder."

"But his career," Hubert Stander stormed, "finished—!"

"Who knows how finished it was, Mr. Stander? The public has a short memory. And King sure must have had enough dough stashed away to keep him going till he could ease back in." Trimble turned to Nancy King again. "Your husband admitted to that investigating committee he'd accepted something like half a million dollars in payola over the last four-five years, Mrs. King. And that's all aside from his legit income from TV and records. Would you say he had any financial worries?"

She looked up. "I can't tell you, Sergeant."

"Oh, come on, Mrs. King."

"I can't. Tutter never discussed his finances with me."

Trimble said in a dry voice, "Wives have been known to ask."

The merest suggestion of life invaded her face. "I wasn't that kind of wife."

"Sounds like Tutter wasn't that kind of husband, either," Winterman remarked.

"He was a very good husband to me, Sergeant Winterman!" There was actually animation in her voice. "There wasn't anything I ever wanted that Tutter didn't give me, cheerfully. I always took it for granted, of course, that he was making a lot of money. But how much of it he saved I can't tell you."

"Didn't you save any of it for him?"

She froze. "I think I've answered your question. I don't see why I should answer it again."

Trimble glanced at Winterman, and Winterman nodded. The scarred detective was about to say something to Layton when Hubert Stander said in a fretful voice, "I don't understand you people. You have this ridiculous idea that someone murdered King, yet you haven't done a thing to look for anybody—"

"There are officers posted at the doors of Studio A, and every exit from the building is under guard," Trimble said mildly. "Nobody's going anywhere, unless they went before we got here. Layton."

"Yes, Sergeant."

"You said something about the way this building's laid out. Suppose you show us."

"I think," Layton said, "Mr. Hathaway'd better come along."

The uniformed man remained with Nancy King and Hubert Stander. The two detectives and Layton went out and over to Hathaway's office, Hathaway trailing unhappily behind. Mrs. Grant stopped typing as if she had been shot.

"Mr. Hathaway—" she began in a trembling voice.

Hathaway glared at her, and she swallowed. "Hazel, these are Detective Sergeants Trimble and Winterman. My secretary, Hazel Grant."

"But . . . why come to me?" Mrs. Grant asked. "I don't know anything. Anything."

"Maybe Layton can answer your question," the station manager snapped. "This was his idea!"

Layton ignored him. "Mrs. Grant's desk faces the door to this branch of the hall," he pointed out to the detectives. "Mrs. Grant, I didn't see this door closed once today. Do you usually keep it open?"

"Yes."

"Then you'd be bound to notice anyone passing in the hall, wouldn't you?"

"When I'm at my desk, Mr. Layton."

"Did anyone pass along the hall out there—in either direction—before I showed up during The King's Session intermission, or after I left?"

"The only person besides yourself that I remember seeing

29

was Mr. Stander. He came into the office here and asked for Mr. Hathaway. I told him Mr. Hathaway was in the Studio B and C control room, and he left."

"The only one, huh?" Trimble said thoughtfully.

"The only one I *saw*," Mrs. Grant insisted. "When I'm not at my desk—"

"Well, how many times weren't you at your desk?" Winterman demanded.

She flushed. "As a matter of fact, I didn't leave it."

"Then why didn't you say so in the first place?" Winterman turned to Layton. "That pretty well seals off this end of the hall, all right."

"Let's try the other end," Layton suggested.

They left Hathaway's office and turned into the other arm of the corridor, the one lined with the dressing rooms. The door to dressing room 1 was closed; an officer was lounging outside. Hathaway, Layton noticed, walked past very quickly, as if he were afraid the door might open.

The control room at the foot of the corridor was walled in glass on three sides. Through the nearest of these, as they approached, they could see in and beyond. The other two glass walls, inside the booth, were at right angles to each other—one overlooking a small studio Hathaway identified as Studio B, the other a slightly larger one he said was Studio C. Both studios and the booth were empty.

"As you see, we use the same control room for both B and C," Hathaway explained.

"Which one of these," Trimble asked, "was in use for that ten-minute newscast during The King's Session intermission?"

"Studio C."

"Who was working in the booth here during the newscast?" Layton asked Hathaway.

"Edwards, our chief control engineer, and his two assistants, Spooner and Kent. Spooner is on sound, Kent is on visual—"

"Where are they now?"

"Back in the Studio A booth."

Trimble fingered his glass eye. "I see what you're getting at, Layton. If those three didn't see anyone go up this arm of the hall, that means the only place a killer could have come from was Studio A—up there where the two branches of the hall meet."

"I can assure you," Hathaway said stiffly, "that no one went up this hall during the newscast. I was right here in the control room with Edwards, Spooner, and Kent, and I certainly would have noticed anyone, where they mightn't have."

30

"Where you here from the beginning of the newscast?" Layton asked.

"Not from the very beginning—"

"Then how do you know someone didn't dodge up the hall before you got here?"

"Are you a reporter or a detective?" Hathaway snapped. "It so happens that just after I stepped out of my office in the other corridor to walk down here for the newscast, I saw Tutter King, very much alive, come out of Studio A, and right after him his assistant, that redheaded girl, Lola Arkwright. King stopped for a second to let the girl catch up, and I overtook them. We all turned down this hall, practically together."

"Oh?" Sergeant Trimble said. "What did King say?"

"To me? Not a word—he hadn't spoken to me since we canceled his show. They walked on ahead of me and then separated. I saw Tutter go into his dressing room and Lola Arkwright into hers. Lola shut her door, and so did Tutter. And I walked on to the control room here." Hathaway tapped the glass wall outside which they were standing. "I couldn't have missed seeing anyone pass to go up the hall."

"Then how come you didn't see anything going on toward the other end there?" Sergeant Winterman growled "Or did you?"

"No!" The station manager was becoming angry. "There's a lot of difference between noticing if someone passed a few feet on the other side of a sheet of glass and noticing something going on forty feet away, Sergeant. I wasn't there for the purpose of *watching* the hall. I had to see Edwards. Then Mr. Stander came into the booth—"

"Just when did you and Mr. Stander leave this booth?" Trimble asked.

"I can't be exact—maybe two minutes before the end of the newscast. We walked back up this hall and into the other corridor together to my office."

"Meet anyone on the way?"

"No," Hathaway said. "I did notice as we passed that Lola's dressing-room door was now open, whereas Tutter's was still closed, but I really wasn't paying attention. I just assumed they'd both gone back to Studio A to resume the Session."

"Then King could still have been alive when you and Stander passed," Winterman said. "The killer could have been right behind you."

"No," Layton said. "When Lola Arkwright asked me to find King, about thirty seconds before the newscast ended, I ducked out of Studio A and had a clear view of both halls. In the other one I saw Hathaway and Stander just going

31

into Hathaway's office. This hall was deserted, and I found King's body in dressing room 1 practically at once. So he must have been killed before Hathaway and Stander left this control room to walk up the hall."

The detectives were silent. Layton could almost hear their minds clicking away at the testimony so far. If it was to be believed, the limits of the murder period were fixed between the time Hathaway saw King and Lola Arkwright enter their respective dressing rooms a few seconds after the newscast interval began, and the time Hathaway and Stander together left the newscast control room to walk back up the hall—a period of seven or eight minutes.

Layton almost grinned when Sergeant Trimble suddenly said, "Mr. Hathaway, you say that while you were on your way to this control room—when you met King and Miss Arkwright heading for their dressing rooms during the intermission—you saw the girl shut her door but King leave his open?"

"No, no, Sergeant, I said they were both closed. Why do you ask?"

"Just trying to see a pretty complicated picture, Mr. Hathaway."

Neat, Layton thought. By phrasing his question around Lola Arkwright, Trimble had covered up his real purpose, which concerned Hathaway. Trimble was thinking, Layton knew, that after Lola shut her door Hathaway himself could have stepped into King's dressing room, stabbed the disc jockey, walked out, shut King's door, and continued to the Studio B and C control room without the loss of more than a few seconds.

Mentally, Layton apologized to the scarred detective for spoiling his theory. "The only thing is, Sergeant," he said, "King wasn't stabbed in his dressing room."

Trimble whirled on him. Winterman, who had been sucking on a toothpick, lowered it in surprise. "What do you mean, Layton?" Trimble said. "You seem to know a hell of a lot about this! He was stabbed somewhere else and dragged to his dressing room?"

"I don't mean that at all. I mean that dressing room 1, where I found King dead, *isn't* his dressing room. Mr. Hathaway, King's dressing room is number 2, across the hall from 1—am I right?"

"Certainly," Hathaway said. "Didn't you people know that?"

"I'll be damned," Winterman said.

"Now they tell me!" Trimble took off with lunging strides, his good eye glittering balefully.

One of the police laboratory men said, "It's an ice pick, all right, Harry—the ordinary varnished pine-handle type. The only fingerprints on it are King's."

"What did I tell you?" George Hathaway cried from the hall. The body was still on the floor, lying like a dummy in a chalked outline, and the station manager had taken one look, swallowed, and stepped back. "He killed himself! What better evidence could you want, Sergeant?"

"You give up easy, Mr. Hathaway," Trimble growled. "I can think of lots better evidence. A dying man will do funny things. King's prints could have got on the handle if he'd tried to pull the ice pick out of his chest—after somebody else put it there." Hathaway muttered something, and Trimble turned back to the lab man. "How does it stack up for suicide, Lew?"

The technician shrugged. "The angle of thrust is okay for a self-inflicted wound—if it was self-inflicted."

"Any hesitation marks?"

"No, but you know, Harry, that doesn't rule suicide out. I've seen plenty of suicides determined enough to plunge the blade in nice and clean on the first try. And ice picks go in like into cream cheese."

Trimble grunted. "I just found out this isn't King's regular dressing room, Lew. His is number 2, right across the hall. Better go over that, too."

"By the way," Sergeant Winterman asked Hathaway, "just whose dressing room is this?"

"Nobody's in particular, Sergeant. It's given to guest stars, usually—they all like that number 1. Today it's been unoccupied."

Layton and Hathaway tagged after the two detectives as the Homicide men headed for Hubert Stander's office.

"Seems to me this is awfully sloppy police work," the station manager mumbled. "Where's the police doctor?"

"In the movies," Layton said. "The body will be examined by a doctor from the coroner's office at the Hall of Justice."

"The Hall of Justice?"

"In the basement there. That's where the morgue is."

They reached the board chairman's office just in time to hear Sergeant Trimble say to his partner, "Get that Arkwright woman in here, Ed."

Winterman held his wrist up to his eyes in the gloomy board room; the Venetian blinds were still closed. "The show has eighteen minutes to go yet, Harry." He grinned. "Want I should bust in?"

"We're still on the air!" Hathaway yelped. "You can't do that!"

33

Trimble glowered, evidently tempted. But then he said, "All right, we'll wait."

Nancy King was on the big couch, her hands folded in her lap, staring up at nothing. Hubert Stander was at the window Hathaway had opened earlier, staring down at nothing.

They all waited.

« 5 »

But after a few minutes Sergeant Trimble became restless.

"About that ice pick," he said. "You don't see many ice picks around these days."

"Well, I never saw it before," Hathaway said defensively, "If that's what you're getting at. Any ice needed in the dressing rooms, or anywhere else in the building, comes in cubes out of refrigerators."

"You ever see an ice pick in this building, Mr. Stander?"

Stander turned from the window. "What Sergeant?"

Trimble repeated his question. Stander did not even bother to reply. He shrugged and turned back to the window.

"How about you, Mrs. King?"

"I wouldn't know."

"Could your husband have brought one here from home?"

"We've never had an ice pick. Unless . . ."

Trimble glanced at Winterman, and Winterman said, "Unless what?"

"Unless he brought it from his apartment in Hollywood." She seemed to feel a need to explain. "You see, that was necessary—I mean, Tutter's maintaining a separate apartment. Our house is out in the Valley, but he had to have a place where he could pretend to be a bachelor."

"Did he have an ice pick in the Hollywood apartment, Mrs. King?" the one-eyed detective asked.

"I can't say. I've never been in it."

The lovely, expensive voice told nothing, nothing at all. She's had plenty of practice covering up, Layton thought. What a heel King must have been to make her lead a life like that. Layton had a sudden vision of Lola Arkwright leaning across the table in King's dressing room and cupping his boyish face. I'll bet the redhead knows her way around King's Hollywood apartment, he thought grimly.

34

"What, Sergeant?" Layton said.

Trimble was eyeing him curiously. "I asked you if you'd seen an ice pick in King's dressing room—number 2—when you had that talk with him before the show you told me about."

"I didn't notice one."

Winterman said, "Wait a minute, Harry. There must be a prop room here. Prop rooms store all kinds of junk."

"Is there an ice pick in your prop room, Mr. Hathaway?" Trimble asked.

"How the devil would I know?" Hathaway said irritably. "Ed, find out."

Winterman went out, shutting the door. Nobody said anything. When Winterman returned, he said, "Yeah, they've got an ice pick, but it's still there, the guy says."

"Better have one of the men check."

The swarthy detective made a face and went out again. When he came back the second time he said, "Say, the Arkwright babe ought to know, Harry. I mean about if Tutter kept an ice pick handy. She seems to've been on what Layton here would call 'intimate terms' with Tutter-boy."

Layton, watching Nancy King, could have walked over and gladly punched Winterman's ugly nose. It was all part of the game, he knew, this deliberate baiting of the principals at the start of a suspected-homicide investigation; but there was something about this woman that touched Layton in a spot he had never known existed. Her only visible reaction to Winterman's foul blow was a slight quivering of her hands, immediately controlled. She was denied by King's cruelty even the ordinary female luxury of showing jealousy.

Trimble changed the subject. "We may as well get a clear picture of the situation during the newscast, as long as we have to mark time here. Let's see, we know your movements, Mr. Hathaway . . . Oh, Mrs. King. Where were you when your husband's show stopped for the news break?"

"In the studio, Sergeant."

"Studio A."

"Yes. When Tutter left at the break, I decided to go back to his dressing room to see him—he hadn't noticed me sitting there."

"How soon after he left the studio did you leave?"

"Oh . . . a quarter of a minute or so."

"Was he in his dressing room?"

"I don't know. I mean, I knew of course that his room number was 2, although this is the first time I've actually been in the station. His door was shut." She colored the palest pink. "I . . . decided not to go in, after all. Even though it was his last telecast, he might have been upset to see me here, and he still had the balance of his show to do. Anyway, I returned to the studio."

"Anything special you wanted to see Tutter about?"

She shook her head. "Just to let him know I was here. As I say, I decided not to bother him till after the show. I didn't think Tutter would be upset when it was all over. After all, it *was* his last show." She stopped, apparently surprised by what she had said. "His last show," she repeated slowly. "That's very funny."

No one laughed. As for Layton, he was engaged in looking into himself. This was something he had been shoving to the bottom of his mind ever since it had happened. What's the matter with me? he thought. Don't tell me Footloose and Fancy-free Layton is falling for a pair of big eyes!

So it came out of him defensively, with a sneering inflection. "I happened to notice you leave the studio after your husband, Mrs. King. It couldn't have been more than twenty seconds or so later that I went out the same door. I didn't see you. Anywhere."

Even the distinguished chairman of the board turned around at that.

Nancy King became aware suddenly of the eyes and the silence. Her face turned Layton's way, and it seemed to him she was seeing him really for the first time. He could have bitten his tongue off.

"How about that, Mrs. King?" Trimble said in a neutral voice. "You said just now you found your husband's dressing-room door closed, you didn't go in or even look in, but went back to the studio. How is it Layton didn't see you?"

Her voice was as neutral as the sergeant's. "Probably because Mr. Layton couldn't see through the door of the ladies' room. I didn't think it necessary to mention that I stopped into the ladies' room—next door to Studio A—on my way back. Are you satisfied, Mr. Layton?"

Through his self-disgust Layton had a wry recollection of his original theory about Nancy King's disappearance. She had been in the women's john, after all! Someday, he thought, I'll learn to leave well enough alone.

"I'm sorry, Mrs. King. Of course, I couldn't have known." He thought he saw her lips lift in the tiniest smile, but in the murky room he could not be sure.

Trimble asked abruptly, "While you were out of Studio A, Mrs. King, did you see anyone? Anyone at all?"

"As I stepped out of the studio on my way to Tutter's dressing room I saw that gentleman—I'm pretty sure it was

36

he"—she was pointing at George Hathaway—"going into the control room at the far end of the hall."

"Anybody else?"

"No."

Trimble nodded. "You're next, Mr. Stander."

"I?"

"When did you get here? What did you do?" Trimble was evidently in no mood to cringe before lofty tones of voice.

"I entered the building at exactly four o'clock," the board chairman said huffily. "I remember the time because I glanced at my watch. I went to Hathaway's office. His secretary was on the phone, but hung up to tell me he had gone to the B and C control room. I therefore went there. Hathaway and I were in the booth for a few minutes, then we walked back to his office together."

"On your way *to* the control room, did you see anybody?"

"I noticed Layton going into Hathaway's office just after I left it," Stander said with a remote nod toward the reporter. "I heard or saw no one else until I got near the B-C control room. Then the Studio A employees' door opened back up the hall—"

"Yeah?" Sergeant Winterman said. "You must have pretty good ears, Mr. Stander. TV studio doors don't make any noise."

"Two hundred or so teenagers do, however," Stander said with an icy glare. "I didn't say I heard the studio door. What I heard was the burst of chatter as the door opened —Studio A was off the air for the newscast, and they sounded like a barnyard. I was annoyed, and I turned around. That's how I happened to see those two slip out into the hall."

"Which two?" Trimble demanded, surprised.

"I'm sure I don't know, Sergeant. Two of the teenagers, a boy and a girl. They had no right using that door—it's plainly marked *'Studio Employees Only'*—and I was half-inclined to have them thrown out of the building. But I decided the fuss wasn't worth it, so I went on to join Hathaway in the B-C booth."

"Can you describe them, Mr. Stander?"

"The boy was—oh, seventeen, I'd say, thin, wearing thick glasses. The girl was younger—on the heavy side, rather homely."

"I have a hunch, Trimble," Layton said, "they were the president and vice president of King's Los Angeles fan club. Mr. Stander's descriptions fit."

"Know their names, Layton?"

"Wayne Mission and Nora Perkins."

Winterman glanced at his watch and said, "Harry, the show'll be off the air in a minute. Want me to get those kids and this Lola?"

"You stay here, Ed." Trimble nodded at the uniformed policeman. They went out.

Layton ambled after them. Trimble was a step from the Studio A employees' door when it opened in his face and Lola Arkwright came hurrying out. The hubbub from the studio held an angry, uncertain note. The red-haired girl stopped in her tracks.

"Get those two kids, Mission and Nora Perkins," Trimble said to the policeman. The man went into the studio. "You're Lola Arkwright?"

"Yes. What's wrong? Is something wrong?"

"I'm a police officer, Miss Arkwright. Suppose we go into Mr. Stander's office."

"It's Tutter," the girl said slowly. "It's Tutter, isn't it? Something's happened to him. I knew it—I knew it when he didn't show up for the second half of the show. He never did that before . . ."

Trimble said nothing, nodding in the direction of the board chairman's office. But at that moment the police lab man came out of dressing room 2.

"Oh, Harry, he said. "We lifted a flock of prints in number 2, but that's all. Okay to release the body?"

"Body," Lola Arkwright said. She moistened her thin, sensuous lips. "Tutter's?"

The one-eyed detective looked disgusted. "As long as this half-wit's spilled it, you may as well know now. King is dead with an ice pick in him. Yeah, yeah," he said to the technician. The man shrugged and went into dressing room 1.

Lola Arkwright was staring at the sergeant, but not as if she were seeing him. Her complexion had turned a creamy yellow. Layton, who was watching her closely, was prepared and he caught her as she toppled.

He carried her into Stander's office and eased her onto the big couch. "I'm about ready to hang out my shingle," he complained as he began to chafe her hands. "Would somebody please get some water?"

"Here, I'll help," George Hathaway muttered.

As Layton and the station manager worked over the unconscious girl, the two detectives conferred in low tones. Layton overheard Winterman tell Trimble that the ice pick in the studio prop room checked out. Trimble nodded gloomily.

The first thing Lola said when she came to was, "Give me a cigarette, somebody."

38

Layton lit a cigarette and handed it to her. He reached over to Stander's desk for an ash tray and set it down on the couch beside her.

She took one drag, punched the cigarette out, and leaned back. "We were to be married."

An incredulous voice said, "Who was to be married?"

Lola's head jerked around to Nancy King. "Tutter was going to announce our engagement at the end of the program."

"You poor thing," Nancy King murmured.

Lola continued to stare at her. "You're Nancy?"

"His wife," Nancy said quietly. "So you know about me."

"Sure. Tut and I had no secrets from each other."

"Then may I ask how you could be 'engaged' to a married man?"

"That's simple as hell, sister," the redhead drawled. "Tutter was going to buy one of those quickie Mexican divorces and get you off his back. Then he was going to marry me."

"I don't know what your purpose is in lying," King's widow said, "but that just can't be true, Miss Arkwright."

"Oh," said Lola, "then you know about me, too."

"That you exist? Of course, as Tutter's assistant."

Lola was silent. Then she said, "Hey, Layton. Butt me again." Layton lit another cigarette for her. This time she puffed on it steadily. Stander and Hathaway had retreated to a corner of the board room and were whispering together. The two detectives said nothing. Nancy King retreated into her thoughts again.

"So you knew I existed," Lola said at last, regarding the widow through narrowed eyes. "Look, honey, if anybody's playing potsie around here, it's you. Tutter hasn't lived with you for years. I'll bet you've forgotten what he looks like, husband-wise."

"Stop her," Nancy cried. "Why must I sit here and listen to this woman's filth? Tutter and I have—I mean, had a home in the San Fernando Valley . . ." She choked and swallowed, hard. Layton saw tears tremble in her eyes.

"That's where *you* live," Lola Arkwright said. *"He* lived in Hollywood."

"Mrs. King," Sergeant Trimble said.

Layton watched her fight once more for control. This time the fight showed plainly. But she won.

"Yes, Sergeant." Her voice was pallid again, like her coloring.

"You said before that King maintained a Hollywood flat to keep up that bachelor act of his, and that you'd never been in it." Trimble's one eye managed to convey sympa-

39

thy. Layton knew that Trimble had about as much sympa-
thy in his make-up as a Siberian wolf. "How often was he
in your Valley house?"

"As often as he could be," she said.

"How often was that?"

"More often than not. I can't give you percentages, Sergeant." The two liquid-dark eyes met the one bleak eye and
refused after that to look away. "I know you don't understand, especially after what Miss Arkwright's said. Of
course we had an unconventional marriage. But we were
happy together. Tutter loved me. All those starlets he was
seen with were publicity stunts. His bachelor apartment was
just part of his public image. Also, he had to have an address for his business and professional friends to come to—he
couldn't bring them home . . . to the Valley, I mean . . .
without their finding out about me.

"We had our own social life. We had friends whose
homes we visited and who visited ours. Good friends, who
understood and were willing to keep his—our secret."

That old devil Slip-of-the-Tongue, Layton thought. Of
course. It was Tutter who'had wanted it that way, not she.
She had hated every minute of it. What woman wouldn't?

Winterman said with a deliberate grin, "Sounds like a
hell of a married life to me."

"No," Nancy said in a tired way. "It was just an incon-
venient one, Sergeant. When we did have each other, it was
very special . . ." The voice faltered. "And now, just when
we could start living normally, my husband's been taken
from me. It isn't fair. It isn't right!"

She burst into tears. Sobbing, she jumped up and ran into
the washroom, banging the door.

Trimble and Winterman looked at each other. For a moment no one said anything.

Then Lola Arkwright tamped out Layton's cigarette.
"Well!" she said with an uncertain smile. "The gal sure has
talent. Anybody here believe that performance?" And without any warning at all, she began to cry, too.

Hubert Stander threw up his hands and stalked into the
outer office, muttering something uncomplimentary about
women. Hathaway hurried after him. Winterman strolled
over to the doorway, where he could keep an eye on them.

"Whenever you're ready, Miss Arkwright," Trimble said
dryly, "let's talk about you."

« 6 »

The red-haired girl blew her red-tipped nose into a hand-kerchief and said, "Excuse me for going female on you. It hit me all of a sudden that Tutter's really dead. And that lying dame in there . . ." She said abruptly, "What do you want to know, Sergeant?"

"About your movements during the intermission," Trimble said.

"Go to hell," Lola Arkwright said.

The one detective eye sharpened. "What are you trying to do, make it easy for me?"

"Look," she snapped, "if you think I knocked off Tutter, stop making like Sherlock Holmes and say so. I don't know who killed him, or why—or even if it was murder. All I know is I had nothing to do with it."

Trimble waited patiently. Winterman, in the doorway, was grinning his head off.

"Now will you answer my question, Miss Arkwright?"

Lola shrugged. "Okay. I spent the intermission in my dressing room, period."

"Was that what you usually did at the news break?"

"Depended on Tut's mood. He wasn't the calm and re-laxed guy he always seemed on the air. Doing a two-hour show five days a week for five years is no picnic. Sometimes Tut wanted to be let alone during the break, sometimes he felt like yacking."

"Never mind him," Trimble said. "I'm asking about you."

"I'm telling you. I always knew how he was feeling by the way he acted as soon as he finished his intermission patter. If right away he jumped off the stand and headed for the door, he wanted to be alone. If he waited for me in the studio, we'd go out together and spend the ten-minute break either in his dressing room or mine. Today he didn't wait, so I knew it was one of those I-want-to-be-alone days."

"But you followed him out. Right out."

"It had nothing to do with him," the girl said wearily. "I just wanted to get to my dressing room."

"How come if it was one of those I-want-to-be-alone days," Layton interrupted, "Hathaway says he saw King stop in the hall and wait for you to catch up?"

41

Trimble and Winterman both glared at him. But the red-head seemed merely surprised. "He did, didn't he?" she said slowly. "That's funny. He almost never did that on one of his bad days. I wonder why he did it today."

"Hathaway says you and King walked on just ahead of him," Trimble growled, still glaring at Layton. "What did King say to you?"

"Nothing. Not a word. We separated at his dressing-room door—"

"I know all that. Oh, Mrs. King," Trimble said, as Nancy King came out of the washroom. "Would you mind waiting in the anteroom with the others?"

She went out past Sergeant Winterman without a word. Layton saw her sit down in the anteroom, away from Stander and Hathaway, and fold her hands in her lap. She had removed all trace of her tears.

"Miss Arkwright," Trimble went on in a lower voice. "Did Hathaway go on past your dressing room?"

"Hathaway? I couldn't say. My door was closed."

"For all you know, then, Hathaway might have stepped into King's dressing room?"

"I suppose," Lola said listlessly. "Though it hardly seems likely, since they weren't on speaking terms." Then her eyes widened. "Are you suggesting that old refugee from the silent flickers might have killed Tutter?"

"I'm not suggesting anything," Trimble said. "Now about the ice pick we found buried in King's chest. It's the common variety, with a varnished pine handle. You recall seeing one like that around here?"

She shook her head.

"How about at King's Hollywood apartment? Ever see one there?"

"No."

Sergeant Winterman said suddenly, "Your dressing room is right next to King's, isn't it?"

"Yes, number 4." Layton saw her stiffen a bit as she turned to the swarthy detective.

"Hear anything from number 2 while you were in your dressing room? Raised voices, for instance?"

"I don't remember hearing anything."

"Would you have heard—if an argument, say, had been going on in the next room?"

She looked doubtful. "I suppose so. If they were talking loud enough."

Winterman signaled Trimble. Trimble said immediately, "When did you go back to the studio?"

Lola's head swiveled again. "About two-three minutes before the newscast was over."

42

"See anyone in the halls?" This was Winterman again, barking.

"Can't you make up your minds which one is asking the questions?" she said angrily. "You're giving me a stiff neck. No, I didn't see anyone in the halls."

Unperturbed, it was Trimble who asked the next question. "Layton says that about half a minute before you went back on the air you ran over to him and asked him to try and find King. Hadn't you tried?"

"Okay, I'll play," Lola said in a grim voice. "Yes, Sergeant, I tried. On my way back to the studio I knocked on Tutter's door—it was closed—then I looked in. He wasn't there. When I got to the studio I went around checking with everybody in sight about if they'd seen Tutter. By then it was almost air time. I spotted Super-Newsman here, and I sent him hunting for Tut because I knew I'd have to take over the balance of the show if Tut didn't make it. Is everybody happy?"

"Where are *you* going?" the one-eyed detective said suddenly to Layton.

"Curses," Layton said. "I thought I'd get to those two kids before you remembered you sent that cop after them."

"Well, think again." Trimble stalked out into the anteroom followed by Winterman, Layton meekly in their wake. They appeared to have forgotten Lola. The redhead hesitated. Then she went into the anteroom, too.

Trimble opened the door to the hall. The uniformed man was waiting outside with the bespectacled boy and the plump girl. "Okay, kids. In here."

The anteroom began to look crowded. Hubert Stander and George Hathaway were perched on corners of the unmanned secretarial desk. Nancy King was still occupying the chair against the wall. Lola Arkwright had chosen a chair at the opposite wall. The two detectives and the two teenagers faced one another in the middle of the room. When the policeman went out at Trimble's nod, Layton leaned against the door. He was wondering why the one-eyed sergeant proposed to question the boy and girl in the hearing of the others; but then he remembered that Trimble had a departmental reputation for doing the unorthodox. Maybe he was playing a hunch.

"You know what's happened?" Trimble asked the teenagers. His voice was very friendly.

"Yes, sir." Wayne Mission swallowed, the Adam's apple in his thin neck jumping like a fish. He seemed fascinated by Trimble's scar. Nora Perkins, pressed against the boy as if for protection, was staring at Trimble's glass eye. "Tutter's committed suicide."

43

"Oh?" Trimble said. "Where'd you hear that, Wayne?"

"It's all over the place," the boy said. "Why, isn't it true?"

Trimble glanced over at Hathaway and Stander. The two station executives returned the glance defiantly.

"It could be," the detective said in a kindly way. "We're not sure. Is something the matter, Nora?"

She blanched and looked away, guiltily. "No, sir!"

"It's the eye, isn't it?" Trimble said with a smile. "Don't worry about it, Nora—I don't give it a thought any more. I know it makes me look like a monster from outer space, but I'm just a policeman doing his job. It was my duty once to stop a fight between a drunk and his wife. The ax he was aiming at her got me instead. No," he went on, turning back to the boy, "we're not sure just how Tut died. I thought maybe you two could help us."

Layton could only admire Trimble's technique. By adopting a fatherly tone and couching his explanation of the scar and the glass eye in modest terms, he evoked a hero image calculated to gain the teenagers' confidence. Layton realized suddenly how desperate Trimble must be for a lead.

"Well, sure, sir," Wayne Mission said. "Anything!"

"If we only *could* help," Nora Perkins said fervently.

"Maybe you can, kids. I understand you both left Studio A through the employees' door during the newscast intermission. Where were you going?"

"To Tutter's dressing room," Nora said promptly.

"You knew him that well, did you?"

"Oh, sure," young Mission said. His voice held a note of sad pride. "Nora and I are president and vice president of Tutter's L.A. fan club—I mean, I'm president and she's vice president. So Tutter allowed us special privileges. We often went back during the news break to talk to him."

"Did you find him today?"

The boy shook his head. "He wasn't there."

"We figured he was in Lola's dressing room," Nora chimed in, "but of course we wouldn't dream of going in *there*."

Lola Arkwright's head jerked to attention.

"No?" Trimble asked in a surprised way. "Why not, Nora?"

The teenagers immediately looked down at the floor. The boy muttered something to his companion, and her plain face flushed scarlet.

"You know, kids," the one-eyed detective said gently, "I don't like embarrassing people any more than you do. But after all, Tutter *is* dead, and we've got to find out everything we can. Why wouldn't you dream of looking for Tutter in Miss Arkwright's dressing room, Nora?"

"Wayne thinks I oughtn't to say," the girl mumbled.

"Why not, Wayne?"

It was the boy's turn to flush. "Well, sir . . . it's kind of disloyal to Tut."

"What they don't want to tell you," Lola said unexpectedly, "is that one time, when they came back during the break—months ago—and looked for Tut in my dressing room, they caught us kissing. Big deal."

"You ought to be ashamed of yourself, Miss Arkwright!" Nora Perkins said indignantly. "Admitting a thing like that right out in public!"

"And what's more," Wayne Mission added, "you got Tut mad at us. He wouldn't let us visit him during the break for weeks after that."

But Lola was not listening. She was staring in bitter triumph across the anteroom at Nancy King.

"I suppose my husband was as vulnerable as any other man would be," Nancy said slowly, "to the advances of an attractive tramp. But it wouldn't have meant anything to him. Not really."

Lola was on her feet, her face as flaming as her hair. "You—calling—me—a *tramp?*"

She sprang—

Sergeant Winterman's simian arms wrapped themselves around her just in time to keep her razor-edged fingernails from raking Nancy King's pale face. The woman with the massed black hair had not moved a muscle.

"You wouldn't want me to run you in for attempted assault," Winterman said, holding the redhead fast. "Come on, stop it before I learn to like it."

As suddenly as she had sprung, Lola Arkwright went limp. And pale, like Nancy King. Winterman cautiously released her. She bit her lip and turned away.

The teenagers were looking stunned. The Perkins girl said to Nancy King, "Did you say . . . your *husband?*"

"Yes," Nancy said, as if nothing had happened.

"*Tutter?*"

She nodded. The girl's unlovely jaw dropped.

"Tutter and Mrs. King have been married since you were about six years old, Nora," Layton said. "He kept it a secret for professional reasons."

The teenager shut her mouth with a snap. Then she said in an outraged voice, "How do you like that, Wayne? To think Tutter would do a thing like—*that!*" She might have been speaking of cannibalism.

Young Mission nodded in a dazed way.

So long, Tutter, Layton thought. You committed the unpardonable sin. He began reshaping in his mind the follow-up story he had to phone in, while he kept one ear mechanically open. Trimble was establishing that the teenagers had noticed Hubert Stander, as they came out of Studio A, walking down the hall toward the control room of Studio B and C; that they had actually seen him enter the control room; t' at they had returned to Studio A after finding King's dressing room unoccupied.

"We're going to release you people now," Trimble was saying. "But please remember we've got an open book on this one, and nobody here is to leave Los Angeles without checking with me first. Give your addresses to Sergeant Winterman."

While they clustered around Winterman, Layton murmured to Trimble, "Does this mean you've decided it's homicide?"

Trimble smiled bleakly. "This means I don't know what it is. Yet."

Layton went into the board room and shut the door. He called for an outside line and spent a long time with the rewrite man in the *Bulletin* city room, angling his follow-up story.

"You seem to have got the jump on the whole town, Jim," the rewrite man said. "I saw the boss a few minutes ago with a contortion of the features that might actually have been a smile. Why don't you hit him for a raise while he's feeling human?"

"The feeling won't last that long," Layton said, and hung up.

The anteroom was empty. He ran out into the hall.

She was waiting just outside the door.

For me? Layton's heart jumped. For God's sake, he said to himself angrily.

"Oh, Mrs. King," he said, smiling, "I thought you'd be gone with the rest."

Her answering smile was faint. "To tell you the truth, Mr. Layton, I . . . don't know what to do with myself. I was just standing here trying to figure out where I go from here."

"Suppose we figure it out together." He put his hand on her elbow and urged her gently into motion. They began to walk down the corridor. "Did you drive in from the Valley?"

She nodded. "I'm parked on the station lot."

"You look kind of shaky." Touching her was like touching a hot iron. He took his hand away.

46

"I'm just beginning to realize that I'll never see him again."

"You're in no shape to drive all that way. Let's stop in here for a minute."

She permitted him to steer her into Hathaway's office. Hazel Grant had her hat on and was pulling on her gloves. Her hands paused for the briefest moment as she saw them.

"Sorry to bother you, Mrs. Grant," Layton said. "This is Mrs. King. She'd like to leave her car on the lot tonight. Could you arrange for someone to deliver it to her in the Valley tomorrow?"

The blue-haired secretary surveyed King's widow calmly. She's not surprised, Layton thought. Did she know all along that King was married? Or had Hathaway just told her?

"We're all so shocked about—what's happened, Mrs. King," Hazel Grant said. "I know there's nothing anyone can say—"

Nancy murmured something.

"I'll be happy to see to your car. If you'll give me a description of it, and the keys and license number . . ."

They were walking across the parking lot before King's widow said anything. "You're very kind to be doing this, Mr. Layton. Whatever it is you're proposing to do."

"I'm proposing to drive you home."

"Oh?" She smiled wanly. "Are you always so masterful?"

"Practically never."

"I'm a good story, is that it?"

"Yes," Layton admitted. "But you're also somebody in trouble. And I've never got over my Boy Scout oath."

She glanced at him—just a flash of the darkly liquid eyes. Then she looked down again.

They walked on in silence.

« 7 »

They got into Layton's shabby car, and Nancy King said she lived on Chapter Drive.

"Where's that?" he asked.

"Near the Valley country club," she said. "I'll tell you when to turn off Ventura. It's about fifteen miles out."

During the first part of the long drive down Ventura Boulevard, she was withdrawn. Almost as if I weren't here, Layton thought, beginning to feel foolish. What the devil did I expect—chit-chat?

47

When they reached Encino he cleared his throat. "It's after six. How about something to eat?"

She shook her head. What a damfool thing to suggest! Layton told himself savagely. He stepped on the gas. But as they approached Tarzana he became aware, in a sort of panic, that she was—very quietly—crying.

"Wouldn't you like to stop at least for a drink?" he asked in desperation.

"I'm sorry." For an instant she touched his arm with her slim gloved hand. Then she fumbled in her bag and brought out a ridiculous wisp of handkerchief and dabbed at her eyes. The faintest of scents invaded his nose. "This is pretty selfish repayment for your kindness. Thank you, but I'd rather get home."

Layton felt confused. He never felt confused. What in the world is happening to me? he thought. He tried to think of something to say, but his brain seemed wrapped in fog.

"Selfish?" he finally said.

"The tears are more for me than for Tutter, I'm ashamed to say. I was feeling sorry for myself because I'd so looked forward to a new life together."

"Aren't all tears selfish?" Layton said fatuously. "You don't have to feel guilty, Mrs. King."

"How do you stop?" She stared at the thinning traffic. "I keep thinking how unfair it is that it should happen just now. It wouldn't have been nearly so overwhelming if Tutter had died before this payola nightmare came up. At that time I had no real hope of our living like normal married people." Her hands convulsed for a moment. "And now you'll think me dreadful."

"I think you're honest," Layton heard himself saying, in a warm tone. "I'd say you've earned the right to feel cheated after all these years of being hidden away like a—like a doll in a closet." Like a doll in a closet! The next thing I know, he thought, I'll be spouting poetry. He struggled to reassert the reporter in him. "Mind if I ask you a personal question, Mrs. King?"

She glanced at him. "It depends on the question."

"Why did you put up with that invisible-wife routine for so long?"

The attractive widow was silent. After a while she said, "I suppose, basically, because Tutter insisted. As I told those detectives, I don't know how much Tutter was making, but it was obviously a great deal. To protect his income, he said, he had to preserve his public image as a bachelor."

"There's more to it than that," Layton said. "What good

48

was the money to you when you couldn't enjoy the life it forced on you? Or was the money an end in itself?"

He had not intended to say that, and he was not surprised when her tone turned cold. "I'd have lived with Tutter in a bungalow court, Mr. Layton. But he wouldn't have been happy." Then the ice melted. "I can't blame you for thinking that. These *are* expensive clothes. The fact is, I loathe the kind of social life Tutter had to lead in Hollywood. I was actually glad not to have to be part of it. We had our own close friends."

Apologies. But, all of it. The real reason she let him make a prisoner out of her, Layton thought bitterly, was that she loved the bastard. Why didn't she say so?

He shook his head clear and promised himself that there would be no more nonsense.

"What flogs me is how you two managed to keep your marriage out of the papers all these years," Layton said in flat tones. "Didn't he ever take you out?"

She sensed his change of mood, and it seemed to puzzle her. "Often. But it was always to out-of-the-way places where we wouldn't run into the Hollywood crowd or the teenage autograph hounds. Sometimes, of course, it didn't work. When he had to introduce me to somebody he knew, he'd say I was his sister."

"His sister!" Layton gripped the wheel. "And you took *that?*"

"I'd have taken anything Tutter dished out, Mr. Layton," she said in a quiet voice. "Better slow down. We're near my turnoff."

At her direction Layton turned left off Ventura.

"It's still a little way," Nancy King murmured, smiling. "Aren't you sorry now you volunteered to take me home?"

Layton mumbled something, and she gave him another puzzled look.

He was soon wrestling the curves at the edge of the Santa Monica Mountains, where Wells Drive twisted and turned uphill and down like a roller coaster. When they finally got to Chapter Drive, Layton said politely, "It's isolated, all right."

"Tutter thought it was perfect," she said. "Practically no neighbors, he said, but only a short distance from civilization."

Tutter thought, Tutter said. To hell with Tutter.

The house was one-story, ranch style, built into the side of a hill too small to be a mountain but big enough for city legs. A small level lawn had been gouged out of the hill, too; the inevitable swimming pool, free form, glittered in its green setting like a crazy-cut jewel.

To hell with Tutter and to hell with you, Layton thought as he pulled the old Plymouth up in her driveway. From now on one of the other guys can run with the ball on this one. But he was only mildly surprised to find himself following her into the house when she offered him a drink.

"I don't want you to think I'm a complete ingrate," she said with a smile. She was damn pretty when she smiled. Damn pretty. "What will it be?"

"Bourbon and soda," he said.

He sat down in a beautifully flowing Danish modern chair while she stripped off her gloves on her way to a little gem of a bar. The living room was full of odd, delicate pieces, graceful and functional, unmatched but *simpático;* there were vases and vases of fresh flowers, and an eternal sort of view through the picture window that occupied most of one wall. The room was exquisite. Her taste, of course, not his. Layton refused to grant the late Tutter King taste.

"You'll have to excuse the mess," Nancy said, busying herself at the bar. Layton could see no sign of a mess. "Light on the soda?"

"Please." When she brought him his drink and had sat down opposite him, he said, "Going to keep living here, do you think?"

"Depends." She leaned back, and Layton studied the improbable mass of glossy black hair above the pale, brooding face. Suddenly she took a sip. "I don't know how much Tutter's left me." She laughed. "I don't even know if this house is clear or mortgaged."

"You don't seem to know much of anything where your husband was concerned."

"The perfect wife." She laughed again, and in the middle of the laugh she started to cry again.

Layton sat perfectly still. Tears became her, he decided. A woman *ought* to cry; it emphasized her. It emphasized her most when she did it against a manly chest. I wonder what would happen if I offered mine, he thought. Right now. Then he saw Tutter King lying on the floor of dressing room 1 at KZZX, all the air let out of him by the ice pick. Layton, I always knew you were a heel, Layton said to himself, but this is just plain perversion. The guy isn't buried yet . . .

"Beg pardon?" he said.

"I said it was thoughtful of you to go wandering off somewhere while I acted female again." She set her drink down on a low coffee table and rose. Mechanically, Layton got to his feet, too. "I'd like to show you something, Mr. Layton."

50

"How about Jim?" Layton said. "It's okay. Your husband called me that."

She gave him a startled look. But then she smiled and said, "All right, Jim. But that's a two-way street. Mine is Nancy."

"I know," he said absurdly.

He followed her down a short hall into a bedroom. She's female, all right, he thought. This is where she kept demonstrating it. Now she's got to show me the scene of the marital crime, to prove to me that the crime was recurrent, and what a willing victim she was.

To hell with her, he thought again.

Here the room conformed. The bed was a typical Hollywood enormity of blanched oak, with matching dressers and a vanity. One of the dresser tops displayed a pair of yellowed ivory hairbrushes, men's; a cuff link and stud box; a man's wristwatch, thin and golden . . . Layton turned away. The other dresser had nothing on it but a photograph of Tutter King in a frame also thin and golden. On the vanity stood a clutter of jars and boxes and bottles.

"So?" Layton said curtly.

She crossed the room and opened the sliding panel of one of twin closets. The closet was full of men's suits, sports jackets, sports shirts, slacks, topcoats. More than a dozen pairs of men's shoes were neatly arranged on a floor rack. There were at least a hundred neckties on a tie rack.

"So?" Layton said again.

She left the closet door open and went to the dresser with the men's articles on top. She began to open drawers. Layton saw men's shirts, socks, underwear, accessories; most of them were monogrammed *TK.* When she shut the bottom drawer and rose, she turned to Layton and said, "Now do you see?"

"See what?"

"That the Arkwright girl was simply not telling the truth. If Tutter hadn't been living with me, as she claimed, would he have kept all these clothes here? I'm sure the police won't find half as much when they look over his Hollywood apartment."

"Mrs. King," Layton began.

"I thought it was to be Nancy, Jim." The dark eyes that searched his face had a sudden anxious shimmer.

"Nancy." Layton forced a smile. "You don't have to prove anything to me. I believe you."

"I'm so glad. For a moment . . ." In her earnestness she stepped closer to him and put her hand on his arm. The faint scent she wore filled his head. How do I get out of this? he thought wryly. "During the week he came home al-

51

most every night. He'd even spend an occasional weekend here, when he got fed up with the Hollywood rat race. It's true," Nancy King added reasonably, "that he often didn't get home till quite late; sometimes after midnight. But he was usually home by ten-thirty or eleven; once in a while he'd be as early as nine. And of course he often didn't leave for the station until almost one in the afternoon. So we really had a lot of time together."

A lot of time together! She had sold herself that bill of phony goods; now she was trying to sell it to him. Okay, I'm sold, he thought, I'm sold, I'm sold. How do I get out of here?

Layton stepped back and brought his arm up to look at his wristwatch. Her hand fell to her side. "I'm afraid I'll have to be getting back, Nancy. You going to be all right here—alone?"

"Haven't you forgotten that I've spent a good many years of days and evenings here—alone?" She was regarding him curiously. "Jim, have I said or done something to offend you?"

"Offend me?" He managed to grin. "Of course not. Anyway, a reporter can't afford the luxury of taking offense. Can I help you during the next few days, Nancy? They're going to be rough—the rest of the news hounds, the funeral, and all—"

"I did offend you," she said. She sounded distressed. "I didn't mean to, Jim. It's been so long since anyone's been that kind to me . . . I mean . . ."

"Think nothing of it," he said lightly. "Part of my job."

"Oh," she said.

"If you want me, yell. You can always get a message to me through the *Bulletin*."

"Yes, Jim."

The drink was still in his hand. He drained the glass and looked around for a place to set it down. She took it from him gently.

"Well," he said. "I'll be seeing you, Nancy. Chin up."

"Yes, Jim," she said again. "And thank you. So much."

And that's that, Layton said to himself as he drove away, knowing that she was watching him from her doorway with that same puzzled, slightly anxious look.

He had to tussle with the weak new Layton inside to keep from looking back.

He won, but it took everything he had.

Layton passed up the countless epicurean palaces along Ventura Boulevard which served superb food at superb prices in favor of a homely little Italian restaurant he knew outside North Hollywood, where he could dine just as superbly on a reporter's salary. But tonight the lasagna tasted like rubber cement and the espresso like boiled roofing tar; the only reason he finished the meal was to spare Mama Ludofacci's easily bruised feelings.

He phoned his office before he left. The King case had kicked up a storm, he learned; reporters for rival newspapers were running around wildly, trying to catch up with the *Bulletin;* the big cheese, it seemed, had been overheard to make a complimentary remark about one Jim Layton, an unprecedented event in the *Bulletin*'s history. There was nothing new.

It was only after he hung up that Layton realized he had said nothing at all about the deceased's secret home on Chapter Drive, or that he had just come from a tête-à-tête there with the widow. The realization did not buoy up his sunken spirits.

Later, he found himself surveying his three-room apartment on Seventh, near Parkview, with a sour eye. It had always seemed to him a comfortable, even an attractive, place from which to tell the world to take a flying leap. Now it was all wrong, a flophouse with shabby furniture, bad Modigliani and Dufy reproductions, and a mountain of sterile second-hand books and far-out hi-fi recordings. It was all male, and it all stank.

· Why, for God's sake, Layton thought, I'm living like a pig. Crushed butts in the browned-up ash trays, empty beer cans lying around like corpses, that soiled shirt I forgot to take to the laundry hanging from the three-way lamp—why am I tossing away my hard-earned dough on that drab who's supposed to keep this joint clean?

This angry thought reminded him that Luella might be a drab, but there were plenty of women in the world who could take a dirty flop like this and make something warm and clean and beautiful out of it. And thinking about this untapped supply of female paragons naturally led him to thoughts of the strange, pale, black-topped female living alone in her lovely ranch house remote in the Valley, mourning a skunk who hadn't deserved to lap the lees of her bath water.

At this point Layton abruptly went to bed.

To hell with her!

« 8 »

On Saturdays Layton worked half a day. Early in the morning he phoned Homicide and learned from Harry Trimble that there was still no decisive development in the case. After lunch, on the drive back to his apartment, he suddenly found the prospect of walking into its unkempt emptiness too grim to contemplate. He drove, instead, to the Police Building on Los Angeles Street and parked in the Building lot.

Layton took one of the automatic elevators to the third floor and went down the hall, past the Detective Bureau, to room 314. Sergeant Trimble was sitting at one of the long tables in the squad room studying the contents of an open file folder.

Layton dropped into a chair opposite him, pulled out a pack of cigarettes, and reached over the table to hold it under Trimble's nose.

The one-eyed detective glanced up. "Hello, Layton," he said. He took a cigarette absently, his eye going back to the folder. Layton stuck a match and made for Trimble's nose again. "Oh, thanks," Trimble said. He puffed, began to choke, leaned back, and eyed the cigarette suspiciously. "What are you smoking these days, cubebs? What is this thing?"

"It's a new cigarette named Safe Side. All filter—no tobacco."

"You kill me." Trimble tossed the cigarette into an ash tray and lit one from a pack of his own. "Well? How did you make out with the widow?"

"I didn't know you cared," Layton said lightly. Had they had a tail on her? "Beautiful place she and Tutter built out in the Valley. Full of his stuff, by the way. That Arkwright number was lying her red head off."

Trimble grunted a noncommittal grunt. "Tell me more, Layton."

"There ain't no more," Layton said. "What's on this end? Anything on King since I phoned this morning?"

"I've just been going over the paper."

"Coroner's report?" Layton asked, eying the folder.

The detective closed the folder. "Just an oral one. Inquest is Monday."

54

"Don't I know it. They called me at the shop—I'm a witness. What's the oral report?"

"King died practically instantly—the blade went into his heart dead center. Angle of wound such that it could have been self-inflicted. Unless we turn something up before Monday, the coroner's jury is sure as hell going to bring in a verdict of suicide."

"Do you think it was suicide?"

The detective scowled. "No sign of a struggle, no sign that anybody else was in the room . . . I dunno, Layton."

"The room," Layton murmured. "I ask you, *mon sergeant:* Does a guy leave his own dressing room to walk across a hall and go into an empty one in order to commit suicide?"

"Yeah, there's that," Trimble said. He sighed. "The screwy thing about this case is that, if it was murder, a lot of people had the opportunity to commit it. Each one passed those dressing rooms *alone.*"

"Except the two kids."

"And they could be in cahoots." A grin lifted Trimble's scar and made his glass eye glitter in the shaft of light. "Even you were alone in that hall, Layton."

"Me?" Layton said, astonished. "You mean I'm a suspect?"

Trimble laughed outright. "No motive. We know you never met King before yesterday afternoon. Unless you've got a thing about disc jockeys."

"Mad about them?" Layton asked hastily.

"Anyway, you were there on an assignment. We checked with your editor."

"Thanks, pal!"

"We also checked," Trimble said with a shift of tone, "we also checked into Mrs. King's and Lola Arkwright's backgrounds."

Layton said casually, "And?"

"Seems both were telling the truth about their relationship with Tutter."

"How can that be? Their stories contradict each other. One of them has to be lying, Trimble, and it's obvious that it's Lola—"

"No." The detective stopped.

"Go on."

"No," Trimble said again. "You're too damn easy to talk to. Nice to have seen you, Layton." He stubbed out his cigarette.

"Look, Sergeant," Layton snapped, "I was in on this from the start. From before the start! I figure that entitles

55

me to the inside track. Besides, you and I share something on this case."

"What?"

"We're both pretty sure it's murder. Loosen up, Trimble. Maybe we can help each other on this one. It's Saturday afternoon, and you know what that means—I'm here on my own time. So I can play it any way you say."

Trimble's one eye speared him "I'm probably going soft in the head to trust one of you bastards," he said suddenly. "But all right." He leaned forward planting his huge palms on the table. "It's King who was lying. To both women."

Layton said softly, "The double-life bit."

"That's it." Trimble opened the folder. "This is a report just in. Two couples out in the Valley back up Mrs. King's story—she and King *have* been living as man and wife in that Chapter Drive house right up to yesterday, and these friends of theirs say they never saw any evidence of marital trouble. And here's a report on the Arkwright girl. Friends of hers bear out *her* story. They say King and Lola have been cozying up for months. She bragged to her friends only a few days ago that he was going to marry her as soon as he got certain personal matters straightened out. The friends took it for granted Lola meant the mess he was in because of the payola scandal. They didn't know King had a wife."

"Lola knew."

"But not that he was still living with her—Lola claims he'd told her he hadn't had anything to do with his wife in years, and I believe her. It's my hunch this Lola broad's been steering King toward a preacher for a long time, and he told her he had a wife in self-defense. But the guy got himself in a bind between the two women, maybe one he couldn't wriggle out of. It's sure going to look that way to the coroner's jury—if the subject comes up at all—and with the payola business and the cancellation of his TV show on top of it, I don't know that I'll blame them if they bring in a verdict of suicide." The scar writhed in a scowl. "But then I think of that surprise statement he announced for the end of the telecast. Would he make a promise like that over the air if he was intending to kill himself during the news break? It doesn't figure."

"It might," Layton said, "if what Lola told you is true— that the surprise was to be his announcement of their engagement."

"That was yesterday afternoon," Trimble growled. "Last night we questioned her again, and she finally admitted she'd only 'hoped' that was going to be his announcement. It turns out he hadn't even hinted to her what he was going

56

to say. In fact," he went on, the scowl again in evidence, "he hadn't really committed himself to marrying her, let alone announcing their engagement. He pulled the same line on the redhead that he used on his wife—he couldn't afford to injure his 'public image' as an unattached dreamboat."

"Then Lola *was* lying yesterday with that talk of a Mexican divorce!"

"It was a lie she'd also talked herself into," Trimble said dryly. "When Tutter's career went up the flue, Lola got a weaseling half-promise out of him that he'd at least straighten out his personal life. Right away in her hot little mind this becomes a quickie divorce and wedding bells. You know how women are."

"No, how are they?" Layton said. "And that takes us back to what King really intended to announce at the end of the show. From some remarks he made to me before he went on the air, it might have concerned the payola scandal."

Trimble looked interested. "In what way?"

"Well," Layton said, "my information is that George Hathaway—and other executives of KZZX—knew all along that King was accepting payola."

"And were taking a cut?" Trimble asked swiftly.

"I didn't say that, Sergeant. Neither did my informant. I don't know."

"Who told you this?"

"Sorry," Layton said. "I promised to protect my source."

Trimble shook his head. "If that's all it was—Hathaway and others knowing King was on the take and doing nothing about it till their hands were forced by the investigating committee's publication of the report—where's the motive for murder? All right, so King accuses them on the air. All they'd have to do is deny it—the word of a group of respected TV executives against the sour-grapes accusation of a self-confessed greased-palm artist." He shook his head again. "I don't buy it."

Layton rose. "Got a make on the ice pick yet?"

"Hardly used, of a type manufactured by a New Jersey company for twenty-five years, national distribution. You can buy one just like it in any dime or hardware store in town."

Layton took the Freeway to the Sunset Boulevard interchange. He drove up Sunset to Station KZZX-TV.

The receptionist from the future favored him with a dazzling smile of recognition. Today he was not dazzled. He returned her smile for business reasons. It got him past her desk.

Hazel Grant was distant. "Mr. Hathaway's left for the day."

"Know if Stander's around?"

"I haven't seen him, Mr. Layton."

"Lola Arkwright?"

"Miss Arkwright was employed by Tutter King, not by KZZX. She'd have no reason to be here."

"Thanks a bunch, Mrs. Grant."

She did not reply.

Layton tried the board chairman's door. It was locked.

He wandered around the corner and past the dressing rooms—there was a seal on number 1—to the Studio B and C control room. A cooking program was on the air in B. In the booth two engineers sat at the panel while a third man stood behind them, watching. The standing man was tall and thin and totally bald.

On impulse, Layton tapped on the window. The bald man turned around. Layton beckoned, and the man said something to the other two and stepped out into the hall.

"I won't keep you a minute," Layton said.

"It's all right." The bald man grinned. "They do the work. I'm an executive."

"Edwards, chief control engineer?"

"By God, I'm famous. How did you know?"

"I'm Jim Layton of the *Bulletin*."

"You were the news hawk here yesterday during all the excitement!" Edwards shook Layton's hand fervently. "What's the latest lowdown on the King case?"

"It looks as if the official verdict's going to be suicide."

The engineer shook his gleaming head. "I guess that payola thing busting wide open was too much for King. Though I'd never have said he was the kind of guy who'd put out his own candle."

"Oh," Layton said, "then you don't think it was suicide?"

"I guess it must have been if the cops think so. They sure tore this place apart yesterday, and everybody in it, from Mr. Stander and Mr. Hathaway on down."

"Say, that reminds me," Layton said. "Talking about Hathaway, I mean. He said yesterday he'd come to this booth to see you, Edwards. During the newscast. What was that all about?"

The engineer's expression turned wary. "Why don't you ask Hathaway?"

"Because he's left for the day, and I didn't think of it till just now. What was it, top secret or something?"

"Well . . ." Edwards glanced around, grinning. "We did

58

have general instructions yesterday for everybody to cooperate with you, and nobody's rescinded the order. He wanted me to brief my control team in Studio A about the last few minutes of The King's Session telecast."

"How did he mean?"

"That announcement of King's at the start of the show that he was going to make a special statement just before the signoff—it bugged Hathaway. He heard it on the monitor in his office and hotfooted it down here during the newscast to tell me what to do when King started his statement. If I even suspected he was going to say something derogatory about KZZX or anyone connected with it—zooey! —I was to cut him off the air."

"Did Hathaway give you any idea of what he was afraid King might say?"

"No, and I didn't ask. He's been blowing his top like an overloaded boiler every hour on the hour the past few weeks." Edwards grinned again. "Me, I'm chicken. Mine not to reason why."

"I know what you mean," Layton said sympathetically. "I don't suppose his disposition was helped any by that payola mess."

"It went sour long before that." Edwards looked around again. "Wife trouble," he said in a low voice.

"Oh, yes," Layton said wisely.

"I suppose you know all about it, but what you may not know is that she kicked Hathaway right out of the house."

"No!" Layton said. "She did?"

"I met that bitch once," the engineer said. "God knows Hathaway's no bargain, but a dame like that would drive any man nuts. I hear she's accusing him in her divorce complaint of everything from sodomy to making burnt sacrifices."

They chuckled companionably together.

"Well, I won't keep you from your work any longer," Layton said, "—Tom, isn't it?"

"Hal."

"Sure—Hal. Been wonderful talking to you, Hal."

"Any time, Jim."

They shook hands like old buddies. Layton maintained his stroll until he was out of eyeshot. Then he began to sprint.

The Hathaway House was on Carmelita Avenue in Beverly Hills. It was a manorial two-story brick set in barbered lawns, with formal flowerbeds surrounding an Italianate fish pool. A colored girl in uniform answered Layton's ring. He told her who he was and asked to see Mrs. Hathaway.

The maid left him standing in a black-tiled foyer, very cool and inhospitable. When she returned, she asked him to follow her.

She led him through a silent house to a rear door and a patio garden. Near a barbecue pit with the look of long use stood a verdigrised metal table with a rainbow-colored umbrella over it. Beach chairs were scattered about. A woman in dark glasses, wearing an extreme red bikini, was sunning herself in one of the chairs.

Layton's first glance gave him the impression of youth; her almost entirely exposed figure was trim and firm, and her hair was a lustrous bronze. Then he got a good look at her face. They can't do much about the faces, he thought. She had gone through so many face-liftings and neck-flesh treatments that it was impossible to tell what she must once have looked like. She had made a caricature out of what Layton suspected had long ago been great beauty. At close range the bronze hair had obviously come out of a bottle and some of her lower teeth were a denture. She looked sixty-five and might be six or seven years younger.

Mrs. Hathaway removed her sunglasses for a moment to inspect him, and he saw her eyes. For one horrible instant he experienced the shock of recognition. Layton had once interviewed a man condemned to the gas chamber who had slaughtered—with a hand ax—an entire family of seven, including a two-year-old and a three-month-old infant. Mrs. Hathaway had the same eyes.

"Sit down, Mr. Clayton," she said. There was a terry robe lying within reach, but she did not reach for it. "Would you like a drink?" She put her sunglasses back on.

"Layton." Layton smiled. "And thank you." He seated himself at the table in the shade of the umbrella. "Are you having one, Mrs. Hathaway? My mother told me never to drink alone."

She glanced at him—it was impossible to say how, because of the glasses; but no part of her ravaged face smiled in return. "I never touch alcohol. Alice, fix me a limeade. And fetch Mr. Clayton whatever he wants."

"Layton," Layton said again. "Bourbon and soda, please."

The maid said, "Yes, sir," and went into the house. Her pretty, intelligent face was as expressionless as her mistress's.

"I used to drink," Mrs. Hathaway said. "But past thirty a woman has to start counting calories. Did you know that one shot of whisky contains a hundred calories?"

"No," Layton confessed.

"Watch your figure, I've always said, and the men will watch it, too." She stretched lazily, arched her back like a cat, the tight bikini straining. Her large breasts were remarkably untouched by time.

Layton winced. "You certainly can't have any trouble in that department, Mrs. Hathaway," he said.

The dark glasses flashed his way for an instant. "Thank you, Mr. Clayton."

He did not bother to correct her this time. "Well," he said, "I don't want to interfere with your afternoon, so . . . Oh, thank you." He took the drink from the tray the maid offered, and waited until she had gone back into the house again. "What I started to say, Mrs. Hathaway—"

"I know what you started to say. I was wondering when the press would get around to me." The old woman with the young body sipped her limeade. "It's been nearly a month since I filed for divorce."

"Oh," Layton said. "Oh, yes. Yes."

"Of course, neither George nor I has been in the public eye in recent years." She was talking dreamily to the sun, as if through an interpreter. "I naturally don't count that stupid job George has at a desk . . . What I mean is, the public has such a fickle memory. When George and I were stars—and I mean stars, Mr. Clayton, stars of the first magnitude, not the empty faces and feeble little talents that constitute stardom today—when we were right up there at the top, as I say, our breakup would have made headlines from coast to coast."

If this female fossil with the killer eyes had once been a star of the same magnitude as her husband, it was a total surprise to Layton. He studied her profile, trying to detect what it must have been like a third of a century ago, in vain. Who the devil was it that George Hathaway had married? Layton struggled with boyhood recollections of his mother's constant talk of "that divine George Hathaway" —she had been an ambulatory encyclopedia on the subject. But he could not remember.

61

He tried a long shot. "I'm going to throw myself on your mercy, Mrs. Hathaway. I've been trying to recall the name of that last picture you made, and I'm ashamed to say I haven't been able to. What was it again?"

"*April Love,*" she said coldly. "That's fame for you. The critics called it our greatest."

Our greatest. Of course. *April Love* had been George Hathaway's final film. Costarring Linda Norman. This was what had once been Linda Norman. Good God in His heaven. He was a little boy when his mother had taken him to see *April Love*. He could not remember George Hathaway in it at all. But he had never forgotten Linda Norman. This was Linda Norman, the goddess Linda Norman.

Layton closed his eyes. "I remember you so well in it, Miss Norman—I beg your pardon. Mrs. Hathaway."

"Silly boy," the woman murmured; the murmur had a note of physical repletion in it, as if in and by themselves the words "Miss Norman" had constituted a Lucullan feast. "It's so good hearing it again. You know, Mr. Clayton," she went on in that intimate murmur, "I could have had as great a career in sound pictures as I had in the silents. But George and I were planning to be married, and his career ended when sound came in. That eununch's voice of his, you know. It would have crucified George to have me go on, while he fell by the wayside. I was in love with him. So I sacrificed my career."

"I understand," Layton said. He had produced his notebook and was pretending to take notes.

"Money, of course, was no problem," she went on. "That was before the days of the big income taxes and George and I had never squandered our money the way so many big Hollywood stars did in those days. George didn't start throwing his money away—on rotten investments—until after he stopped earning it." Layton had to steel himself to keep looking at her; now it was her smile that recalled the cold-blooded killer he had interviewed. "Lousy businessman, George. About all he has now is his income from that belly-scraping job at KZZX. So I'm not asking him for a thing except this house and its contents. I do hope you understand, Mr. Clayton, that I'm not the kind of woman who sucks a man dry and then divorces him. My money is intact —I don't need his."

Layton was wondering how he could maneuver the conversation around to the real reason for his visit. This was one he'd have to play by ear.

"Do you have any definite plans, Miss Norman," he asked, poising his ballpoint, "for after your divorce?"

He watched that formidable bosom expand again as she breathed deeply. "I may try a comeback," she said.

Comeback, Layton pretended to write, and then he rather desperately took a long pull at his drink. "Now about the divorce, Miss Norman—"

"Do call me Linda, Mr. Clayton."

"If you'll call me Jim." Maybe she'd remember "Jim."

"All right, Jim." She smiled. "I suppose you want to know why I'm suing. Well, George was never easy to live with, but in recent years he's been impossible."

"In what way, Linda?" This was more like it.

"For one thing, he's psychopathically jealous. I can't look at a man that George doesn't accuse me of having gone to bed with him. He's actually beaten me at such times."

"Actually?"

"Actually," she said a little sharply. "Then I began finding lipstick on his handkerchiefs. Of course you see what happened."

"I'm afraid I don't, Linda."

"You men! You stick together, don't you? What's behind all George's jealousy, obviously, is the guilt he feels over his own adultery. He's justifying his infidelities by transferring them to me."

"I see," Layton said respectfully. These do-it-yourself psychiatrists! he thought. "Then Mr. Hathaway has no basis for his jealousy?"

"You're trying to ferret out another man, aren't you, Tim?" she said with another smile. Layton groaned inwardly. He would be Tim Clayton to her until she died. "Well, of course, many men have admired me. I certainly can't help that."

"Certainly not," Layton said in a warm tone.

"The last time I accused George of taking up with some trollop or other," the woman in the bikini went on, "he beat me so brutally I was under my doctor's care for a month. I began to fear for my life. So I locked him out of the house and got a court injunction to keep him out. Have you interviewed George yet?" she asked suddenly.

"Not about the divorce," Layton said. "I saw him yesterday on a different story."

"The Tutter King suicide, I suppose." She shrugged. "When you do interview him about the divorce, he'll undoubtedly fill you full of psychotic lies about me. You know, of course, that he's countercharging adultery with numerous young men. He claims I maintain a whole stable of them—*stable!* That's his word, Tim, as if I were some sort of brood mare or something. He's so *transparent.* He's just making a fool of himself."

63

Layton promptly moved into the opening. "Talking about the Tutter King business," he said, "do you think maybe the strain of the payola scandal and its possible effect on Mr. Hathaway's position at KZZX might have had something to do with his emotional condition?"

"Rubbish," she snapped. "Our troubles came to a head long before that story broke."

"Maybe he knew it was on its way, and the worry—"

"He never mentioned it to me."

"Well, it certainly has him on the ragged edge now," Layton said ruefully. "He nearly chewed my head off yesterday when I asked him a perfectly harmless question."

"That's George," she said, nodding. "So you know what a vicious temper he has. Though I should think the subject of payola *would* upset him." she laughed. "I was so amused when I read that sanctimonious statement he authorized at the time he fired King."

"How come?" Layton asked in a carefully careless tone.

"Because George was as guilty as King. He accepted payola from the record companies, too."

Layton repressed his elation with difficulty. Was it possible she didn't realize the implications of her statement? He decided not to look a gift harpy in the mouth.

"That's interesting," Layton said. "Is he that much of a hypocrite?"

"George? There isn't a sincere bone in his head," she said, laughing again. "What's worse, he's a stupid hypocrite. You'd think if he was going to take payola, he'd make it worth his while. Instead, he accepted peanuts. I don't think the total ever amounted to more than four or five thousand dollars a year. Can you imagine that?"

Layton shook his head. "Unbelievable. What was he supposed to do in return?"

"Nothing," she said indifferently.

"Nothing?"

"He wasn't to interfere with Tutter King's subsidized plugging of certain songs, that's all."

"I get it." Layton chuckled. He was thinking furiously. He decided to take a calculated risk. "I don't want to stray too far from the main purpose of our interview, Linda, but I wonder if this story about Hathaway doesn't tie in with your divorce action. It would certainly make him look bad."

"It certainly would," she said softly.

So she had spilled it to him deliberately. Layton relaxed. He could take off the velvet gloves.

"Yes," he said. "Of course, an unsupported charge of this seriousness, Linda, can't be printed. What I need is proof.

If I had some documentation, the *Bulletin* wouldn't hesitate to plaster it all over the front page."

"What kind of documentation?"

"Correspondence, records, bank deposits—anything like that. Did Hathaway take all his personal effects with him when you sent him packing?"

"He was lucky I let him have his clothes," she said lazily. "I don't know exactly what there is, Tim . . . Suppose I have a look."

"That would be fine," Layton murmured.

The aging woman pattered down the long, curved staircase from upstairs and through the wide archway into her living room with an eagerness as nearly naked as her bikini-clad body. She was carrying a big cardboard box filled with Christmas cards and what looked like letters. She dumped the box on a low tiled table before the huge sofa from which Layton had risen and flung herself into a baroque Italian chair opposite.

"It's all Christmas stuff," she said, "but I think you'll find what you're looking for."

Linda Norman had taken off her sunglasses. The stony eyes were glittering. Medusa, Layton thought, and he went to work.

The cards yielded nothing; among them were many from record companies, but they were the customary seasonal pap. The letters were all on the stationery of different record companies, the majority handwritten—Christmas greetings of a more personal nature from company executives. The rest, also bearing Christmas greetings, were typed. It was among these that Layton struck pay dirt. Some of them went back five years.

One was typed on the letterhead of The Best-Play Recording Company, was addressed to George Hathaway at his Carmelita Avenue address, and read:

DEAR MR. HATHAWAY:

Just a note to wish you a Merry Xmas and a Happy New Year. May you and yours enjoy the holiday season and the coming year in health and prosperity.

Sincerely,
REINHARD K. AULT,
Dir. Publ. Rel.

RKA/nj
Enc.: Check #8271 for $200.

Not all the secretarial typists had made the automatic error of "nj." On some there was no "Enc.: Check #— for

65

$—.—," although Layton had no doubt that in these cases, too, checks for several hundred dollars had been "Enc."-ed with the harmless-sounding message. But there were enough examples of the ironies of secretarial habit to hang George Hathaway several times over.

"You're going to let me have these, Linda, aren't you?"

"With my blessing, darling," the woman said. "They're what you want?"

"They're what I want, all right." Layton tucked the incriminating letters, folded, away in his inside breast pocket.

She smiled, and for a few minutes she chattered on about her post-divorce plans—she might try the movie comeback, she might take a trip around the world instead, oh, she had so many plans, although none of them included remarriage. . . . Layton let her rattle away, on the lookout for an excuse to escape.

It came unexpectedly. The front doorbell chimed, and as the maid passed the living room Linda Norman Hathaway called, "You find out who it is, Alice, before you open that door. Mind?" and Alice said, "Yes, ma'am," and Layton heard the door open and Alice call out—was there the merest touch of malice in her voice— "Oh, it's only Mr. Gerald, Miss Linda. Come in, Mr. Gerald," and before the old woman could get to her feet a young man bounded into the room.

He could not have been more than twenty. Layton had seen scores of him around the Pacific beaches—the deeply tanned, broad-shouldered, hipless blond athletic boys, handsome Nordic counterparts of their darker brothers of the Hawaiian beaches—emotionless, alien to the youth Layton remembered, without conscience or direction, superb male flesh catering to the starved appetites of well-heeled women. This specimen wore the most expensive-looking sports jacket Layton had ever seen.

The boy stopped short at the sight of Layton. He glanced curiously at the old woman in the bikini and said, "Why all the bare skin, baby? It ain't that hot today."

Hathaway's wife was glaring at her maid. Alice vanished.

"Why didn't you phone, Gerald?" the old woman said, sugar-voiced. "I want you to meet Mr. Clayton. Tim, this is Gerald Jacnewski, a friend of my husband and me."

The young man laughed. "Especially of her husband." Before Layton could stir he was across the room and crushing Layton's hand. "That's for nothing," he said. "Now do something."

"Gerald!" the woman said in a furious voice.

Gerald grinned at her and made for the bar.

66

"Well, Linda, I've got to be going," Layton said. "And thanks."

"Thank *you*, Tim. Here, I'll see you out."

Layton lingered outside, blowing gently on his numb hand. Through the open living-room windows he could hear the woman shrilling, "Did you have to show up without warning, you idiot? That man's a reporter!"

"So? It's no bark off my ash," the young man's voice said. "Say, Hot Pants, I got a real cool date tonight and I need some *dinero*. Gimme a hundred."

"Damn you!" Layton heard her cry.

Still blowing on his hand, Layton got into his heap and drove away.

« 10 »

Layton glanced at his watch. It was a few minutes past five. He debated with himself whether to phone Linda Hathaway for the information he wanted and had forgotten. He decided against it.

Instead, he stopped in at a drugstore on Santa Monica Boulevard and phoned KZZX, asking for Hazel Grant. To his relief, she was in. Apparently she worked on Saturday afternoons, too.

"Jim Layton," he said. "Hazel, what's Hathaway's new home address?"

"*You* again," she said. "What did I want to be nice to you for? Mr. Layton, I can't give out confidential information like that!"

"Sure you can, honey," Layton said. "Because I can always get it from Mrs. Hathaway. I have a hunch she wouldn't mind telling me *anything* I want to know about your boss-man."

The phone was silent. Then Hazel Grant said in a venomous undertone, "If you tell him I'm the one who gave it to you, I'll kick you right where it will do you the most good. I mean it. He's in the San Granados Apartments on South McCarty Drive." She hung up so viciously that Layton's ear rang.

The Beverly Hills address was less than a mile from the Carmelita Avenue mansion. It was a tasteless "better-class" apartment hotel with a tiny lobby. A fat young desk clerk sat behind the desk, within reach of a switchboard, reading a comic book.

"Where will I find Mr. George Hathaway?" Layton asked him.

The clerk barely bothered to look up. "In back. Across the court."

"Is he in?"

"Dunno. He usually sneaks in and out through the back way." He set his comic book down resentfully. "I'll ring him. I'm supposed to do that, anyway."

Layton slid a dollar bill across the desk and it fluttered into the fat young man's lap. "Look at all the comic books you can buy if you didn't see me blow by you. How do I get there?"

The bill vanished. "For a buck's worth of comic books I'll give it my personal attention." The clerk grinned. He got up and indicated a short hall leading to the rear of the lobby. Layton followed him.

The hall led to a central court. Across the court an archway opened into a rear alley. On each side of the archway there was a door into the rear building. The clerk indicated the door on the right.

"Through there and up the stairs. You'll find his name plate on apartment 23-E—second door to your left from the top of the stairs. How's that for service?"

"Perfect," Layton said; and he crossed the court, went through the right-hand door, and climbed the fake-Spanish black iron-and-tile stairway. Just as he reached the landing, George Hathaway came out of the second doorway on the left.

"Well, hello, Mr. Hathaway," Layton said. "This is my lucky day."

The KZZX manager peered; the hall was darkish. "Layton?" He seemed disagreeably surprised. "If you're looking for me, I was just going out to dinner."

"This is important, Mr. Hathaway."

Hathaway hesitated. Then he said, "All right," and stepped aside.

Layton found himself in a typical "exclusive" Los Angeles furnished bachelor apartment, consisting of a big flashy room with a wall bed, a recessed kitchenette masked by a mauve plastic fold-back screen, and a tiny bathroom. The furniture was what Layton called "Grand Rapids Swedish Moderne"; there was a television set; there was a small portable bar; a single mass-produced abstract "painting," all blots and doodles, was self-consciously off-centered on one long, otherwise blank wall. The San Granados Apartments, Layton knew, contained scores of almost identical "adventures in living."

"Sit down," Hathaway said ungraciously. Layton sat

down in a back-breaking contour chair; the station manager remained standing. "How did you know where to find me?"

"There are no secrets from the Press," Layton smiled. "Now that that's behind us—"

"Of course, this is only temporary," the handsome old man said. "I had to, ah, move rather suddenly. I wish you wouldn't publicize where I'm living, Layton. You see—"

"Why not?"

"Well, it's only a hundred and eighty a month—with maid service, mind you—but it was all I could get in such short notice—"

"It would bankrupt me."

Hathaway seem mollified. "Can I fix you a drink?"

"No, thanks," Layton said. "I don't drink a man's whisky when I'm going to clobber him."

Hathaway's ruddy cheeks became noticeably less so. "What do you mean?"

"I just came from a long talk with your wife."

The ruddiness dwindled to a milky pink. "I knew you were bad news the minute I laid eyes on you! Well, if you expect a statement from me about my marital affairs, Layton, you're a fool. And I don't think you're a fool. What do you want?"

"Exhibit A." Layton produced from his inside breast pocket a sheet of stationery. He unfolded it and held it up. "I hold here the original of a letter from one Reinhard K. Ault, Director of Public Relations of the Best-Play Recording Company, addressed to Mr. George Hathaway at his former home—"

"She gave that to you," Hathaway said in a choked voice. "She dug that up and gave it to you." He towered over the contour chair with his manicured hands clenched and raised, as if he meant to use Layton's head as a drum. "Give me that letter."

Layton folded it and slipped it back into his pocket in one fluid motion.

"Give it to me or, by heaven, I'll take it away from you?"

Layton crossed his legs very suddenly, and Hathaway involuntarily took a half-step back. "My strength is as the strength of ten because I'm on a reporter's diet. Besides, I'm a generation younger than you, Mr. Hathaway. And while the position I'm in seems to make me a sitting duck, allow me to point out that before you could land a blow you'd be nursing a broken kneecap." His right foot, crossed over his left thigh, was swinging gently. At the top of its arc it came within an inch of Hathaway's right knee.

Hathaway completed the backward step and turned and

went across the room and slowly sat down on the sofa, under the blots and doodles. He leaned forward and put his elbows on his knees and his face in his hands.

"It wouldn't do you any good to muscle Exhibit A away from me, anyway," Layton said. "I have Exhibits B, C, D and so forth stashed elsewhere. They prove, Hathaway, that you've been taking measly but indisputable payola from at least a dozen record companies for five years. Will you please tell me how in hell you allowed them to pay you off by check, and on top of that saved the letters with those ridiculous secretarial 'enclosure' lines?"

The hands dropped; everything in the handsome face was sagging. "Nobody thought it would ever come out. Stupid, stupid. And the letters. I'd told my wife to burn them. I thought she had. The bitch. The treacherous, lecherous bitch!" He looked over at Layton. "I suppose you're going to publish them."

"Not necessarily," Layton said.

The feeblest hope kindled in Hathaway's eyes. "You have a price?"

"Yes."

"What?"

"Your cooperation."

"Cooperation?" Hathaway stared. "In what?"

"In getting at the truth of Tutter King's death."

"What truth? I told you, and I told those detectives, King committed suicide."

"And I told you," Layton said, "I think he was murdered." He got up and began to stroll around the room, hands in his trouser pockets. "I'm going to level with you, Hathaway. I want you to realize the spot you're on. If this was murder, you're a prime suspect."

"You mean you think I killed King?" Hathaway cried.

"I didn't say that. I say the facts now suggest it."

"What facts?" The handsome old man was wholly ashen now.

"You instructed Edwards, your engineer chief at the station, to cut King off the air if he started to say anything nasty about anyone connected with KZZX. The letters your wife gave me show what you might have been afraid King would say. If it came out that you'd been taking payola, too, you'd be out of KZZX on your ear in five minutes. Mrs. Hathaway told me you're broke, that you have nothing but your salary. At your age, and with that kind of public smear—in this town!—what chance would you have of getting another job? I think the police would consider all this a mighty convincing motive for shutting King's mouth."

70

Hathaway said hoarsely, "As God is my witness, Layton, I didn't kill King. If he didn't commit suicide, somebody else killed him."

"Then you tell that to Sergeant Trimble."

"Is that what you meant by cooperation?" Hathaway gripped the edge of the sofa suddenly. "Or am I missing something? You could have taken those letters straight to Trimble. Why didn't you?"

"Because I'm a newspaperman," Layton said, "not a cop. First, I'm giving you a chance to come clean with me—everything you know. I'm after a story—a damn big story, if you ask me."

"I come clean with you, as you put it, and you hang me," Hathaway muttered. "Is that it?"

"Not if you had nothing to do with King's death."

Hathaway was silent. After a while he said, "What about those letters?"

"What about them?"

"Would you use the letters if I can somehow convince you I didn't kill Tutter?"

"It's Sergeant Trimble you'll have to convince."

"So you *are* going to turn the letters over to Trimble," Hathaway said bitterly. "Big deal!"

Layton turned to face him. "Let's understand each other, Hathaway. I've certainly no intention of withholding material evidence from the police. At the same time, if you cooperate, I'll do my level best to keep the letters from being published."

"You wouldn't use them, of course," the TV executive said with a hard laugh.

"I'd be a pretty bum reporter if I couldn't see what a story they'd make. But I'm willing to horse-trade. You give me a better story and I'll do everything I possibly can to protect you."

"A better story." Hathaway mused. Then he looked up. "Keep going," he said.

Layton sat down on the edge of the contour chair, leaning forward. "I'll ask Trimble to sit on the letters. I can't guarantee he will. If he decides to release them, I'm obviously not going to let the other papers scoop me on my own story. In that case, you can be damn sure the *Bulletin* will publish the letters faster than you can lift your leg. But if Trimble agrees to play ball, you're safe."

"For how long?" Hathaway jeered. "So I'll be ruined next week instead of tomorrow."

Layton said patiently, "Not if you're innocent. If Trimble decided to book you for murder, naturally he'd present the letters in court as evidence, to establish your motive. If he

71

doesn't have to use them as evidence, my personal opinion is that he'll go along with my request to keep them in confidence."

It was the station manager who got to his feet this time and paced.

"You've got me hung up by the crotch," he muttered. "If I talk, I'll be fired just as surely as if you'd published the letters."

"Not if you talk off the record. I've never violated a confidence in my life." Layton added, "Always provided, of course, that what you tell me isn't self-incriminating. I won't sit on a confession."

"I have nothing to confess." Hathaway halted to study the reporter. "You'll guarantee not to disclose the source of your information if and when you relay it to the police?"

Layton nodded, "With the aforementioned proviso."

The old man struggled with himself. He sat down again suddenly. "What did my wife tell you about those checks?"

"That they were bribes for not interfering with King's subsidized song plugging."

Hathaway shrugged. "That's true only in effect. Actually, there was never any understanding, written or oral. The checks just started coming. What would you have done? Sent them back?"

Layton said dryly, "You knew what they were for, didn't you? The point is, you kept the money and didn't interfere with King."

Unexpectedly, the old man laughed. "It's almost funny. I couldn't have touched King anyway."

"Why not?"

"Orders."

"From whom?"

George Hathaway said, "Hubert Stander, chairman of the board."

Layton was silent. Then he said, "Stander . . . What was Stander's interest in Tutter King?"

"King plugged his records."

"*Stander*'s records? What are you talking about?"

"Stander owns the controlling interest in the Southwestern Recording Company," Hathaway said with relish. "King gave Southwestern's platters a free ride with the understanding that his payola deals with other companies wouldn't be interfered with."

Layton said softly, "So Stander has secret control of a record company. Wouldn't the FCC regard that as a conflict of interest?"

"You're damned right they would," Hathaway snapped. "At worst, KZZX could have its license suspended, maybe revoked. At best, Stander would be forced to dispose of his interest in either the station or the recording company. Why should the announcement King said he was going to make have concerned me? He had a lot bigger fish to fry. It was Stander he was after."

Layton sat very still. "How far from the station does Stander live?"

"Ten, fifteen minutes at the most. He lives in Beverly Hills, too." Hathaway's eyes were glittering.

Layton pretended not to notice:

"He got to the station at 4 P.M. by his own admission. King had gone on the air at three o'clock and right away announced that he was going to make an important statement at the end of the telecast. With King doing his last show, Stander sure as hell must have been tuned in."

"You bet!" Hathaway said eagerly. "So he had loads of time to drive over to the station. Maybe purposely timing it so that he got there just at the beginning of the news break. That way there'd be less chance of his being collared by somebody on station business, and——"

"And what?" Layton said when Hathaway hesitated.

"You know and what, Layton."

"Then why don't you say it? You think Stander stuck that ice pick into Tutter?"

"I'm not saying that, you are," Hathaway said quickly. "I'm merely pointing out that he had opportunity, and a lot stronger motive than mine."

"The strength of motives, Hathaway, is relative. A starving man might kill for a loaf of bread. For you to keep your job was as strong a motive as for Stander to protect his millions."

"Whose side are you on, anyway?" Hathaway cried.

"You force me to use lofty language," Layton murmured: "I'm on the side of truth."

Hathaway shouted a four-letter word. "You've conned me into this, Layton! You want to know something else? Stander had two motives!"

"Oh?" Layton said.

"Tutter beat his time with Lola Arkwright!"

Layton had to work to keep his voice casual. "I didn't see any sign of a relationship, present or past, in Stander and Lola yesterday. Are you sure you aren't giving me a typical Hollywood rumor as a fact? Stander's old enough to be Lola's father, and then some."

"Where were you born, Layton, under a mushroom? You expect an experienced old lech like Stander and a professional tramp like Lola to betray themselves under the eyes of a couple of detectives in a mess like this? I know what

73

I'm talking about! Stander was paying her rent before Tutter started his show on KZZX. As a matter of fact, it was Stander who introduced Lola to Tutter. The next thing Stander knew she was working Tutter's turntable during the show and his bed after it. Our distinguished friend was all broken up about it—don't ask me why; he must have known all along she was playing him for the usual sucker, who'd leave him the minute someone better came along."

"Better?" Layton's brows rose. "Stander's a multimillionaire. Tutter wasn't in his class."

"Yes, better," Hathaway said viciously. "Right from the start that redhead saw the possibility of steering Tutter into marriage. She couldn't have married Stander in a thousand years."

"Because he's married and has a son older than Lola?"

"No! Because Stander *couldn't* marry her, even if he got rid of that wife of his. Stander's social position means as much to him as his money, and to have made Lola Mrs. Stander would ruin him in that precious 'set' of his. Just the same, as his mistress, Lola made him feel young again, and he was pretty much involved emotionally. It was a real crusher to him when King took her away from him. Yes, I'd say Stander had a double motive!"

Layton rose abruptly. Hathaway kept watching him.

"Where does Stander live?"

"On Crescent Drive somewhere. I don't know the exact address." Hathaway added bitterly, "I'm not on his social list."

"How about the Arkwright girl?"

"Hollywood, I think."

Layton went over to Hathaway's telephone table. He dug out the Beverly Hills book, looked up Stander's address and phone number, and jotted them down in his notebook. Then he consulted the thick Los Angeles directory. There was no Lola Arkwright listed.

"You sure she lives in Hollywood?"

Hathaway shrugged. "That's what I've always understood."

Layton replaced the phone books; Sergeant Trimble had the address and telephone number of everyone involved. He went to the door.

"Wait!" George Hathaway said anxiously. "What about me? What happens now?"

"Sit tight," Layton said; and he left.

« 11 »

Layton was driving past an elaborate edifice set back
from a corner, all glass and swooping roof—Beverly Hills
drive-ins were conceived in the spirit of the Taj Mahal—
when the realized that he was hungry. He turned his jalopy
into the side street and approached the temple of eats on
the bias. Then he killed his engine and tooted.

The goddess of a carhop who came out with a menu and
an attachable tray could hardly conceal her contempt for
the underprivileged vehicle. Layton ordered two super hamburgers and a frosted chocolate and settled back to think.
The goddess took her time returning to the temple, exhibit-
ing an awesome wiggle in her retreat. Layton did not even
notice it.

After thirty seconds he got out of the car and made for
the telephone booth inside. He consulted his notebook and
dialed Hubert Stander's number.

A heavy female voice said, "This is Helga, yah? Stander
residence."

"Is Mr Stander in?"

"Mr. Stander is from town out. Who calls him?"

"When do you expect him back?"

"By the airplane he comes back. Tomorrow morning,
eleven o'clock. Who calls him?" Helga insisted.

Layton hung up. This was interesting. Trimble had
warned Stander, with the others, not to leave town except
by permission. Had Stander checked out with the sergeant,
or had he violated the order?

Layton left the booth and consulted the Los Angeles
directory. Several dozen Trimbles were listed, but no Harry
Trimble. He searched for Trimble's partner, but there was
no Ed-something Winterman listed, either. Apparently the
local passion for unlisted home telephone numbers extended to the gendarmes.

Layton went back into the booth, called the Police Building, and asked for Homicide.

"Homicide Lieutenant Jackson, yes?"

"Sergeant Trimble around, Lieutenant?"

"Who is this calling?"

"Jim Layton of the *Bulletin.*"

The weary voice became guarded. "Trimble's on the day
trick."

"I know," Layton said. "But he's a working fool so I thought—How about Ed Winterman?"

"Same deal, Layton. Catch them tomorrow morning. They both pull Sunday duty,"

"Hold it! Don't hang up on me. You the same Jackson who used to be a sergeant in Robbery?"

The lieutenant's voice warmed noticeably. "It must be a long time since you hung around the squad room."

"Maybe too long," Layton said. "Say, Lieutenant, I can't find either Trimble or Winterman in the phone book. Unlisted numbers?"

"Yeah. Is this important?"

"It's about a case they're working on."

The lieutenant hesitated. "They're at a stag party for one of the Homicide boys who's taking the leap. If it's something that can't wait, I'll ring the party and have one of them call you."

"No, it'll keep. What time does Trimble go on duty tomorrow?"

"The day watch begins at eight-thirty. Trimble's usually early. Try him around eight-fifteen."

"Thanks," Layton said, and hung up.

The goddess was waiting for him with the check. He paid her and picked up one of the super hamburgers. "Hey, lovely!" he said in an injured tone. "This superham is super-cold."

"It was hot when I brought it," she said disdainfully. "You're lucky we didn't charge you rent." And she wiggled away. This time Layton noticed. He watched while he chewed on the cold food.

Afterward, driving along in the thickening Saturday-evening traffic, Layton felt the onset of his usual weekend blues. It was too late to arrange a date; there was nothing more he could do tonight on the King case; and the prospect of curling up in his apartment with a good book, or even a bad one—he had stashed away a paperback edition of *Tropic of Cancer* for just such an emergency—was suddenly without appeal. A movie?

Layton passed a bank clock. Twenty of seven. Automatically he veered off in the direction of Ventura Boulevard.

He was halfway to Chapter Drive in the Valley before he permitted himself to dip deeply into himself.

He had left Nancy King's ranch house twenty-four hours before with everything settled. He remembered his exact thought on driving away: *That's that*, and on going to bed: *To hell with her*. Last night my mind was made up not to see that loving-husband mourner again, Layton thought, except as the developments of the case professionally de-

76

manded. And here I am, like a kid with his first case of she-itis, heading back the next night. What is this?

And what reason could he give for driving all the way out there?

With a shock Layton realized that the compulsion to see Nancy King again had been lurking behind his entire day.

As he swung his car into her driveway, his tires sizzling on the gravel, Nancy backed out of her house and tried her front door. Then she turned around and saw him. She was wearing a dark blue suit and a saucy little matching blue hat with a wisp of half-veil and longish dark-blue gloves.

"Oh!" she said. "Hello, Jim."

Layton's stomach felt hollow. "You were expecting somebody else to be driving up," he said lightly.

"I thought it was the taxi I ordered. How are you, Jim?"

"Didn't they deliver your car from KZZX?"

"Oh, yes. But I'm still not up to driving, I'm afraid I . . . didn't have a very good night."

Through the veil Layton could see the fatigue smudges under her eyes. "I'd be glad to take you wherever you want to go, Nancy. Cancel your cab."

"I'm going 'way downtown."

"Just where I'm headed."

"Liar." Nancy smiled. "All right, let me try to catch the taxi." She unlocked her door and went back in. Layton waited outside in a juvenile glow. She was still smiling when she came out. "He sounded grateful. They hate to send cabs out here."

He helped her into the heap. Her flesh under the sleeve felt warm and yielding, and he quickly let go and closed the door and went around the car and got in and said over-brightly, "Where to?"

"The Everglade Funeral Home. It's on Wilshire, near Lafayette Park"

He nodded. "That's only a short walk from where I live." He started the car and drove off. The glow was gone. She glanced at him once, with the tiniest frown, then looked straight ahead.

Layton drove rigidly. What had he expected? That she was setting out for an evening of bridge the night after she became a widow? *This has got to stop. I'm acting like a lovesick kid. . . .*

He had turned into Ventura Boulevard before Nancy spoke. "I promised Mr. Everglade I'd be there between eight and eight-thirty."

She knows something's wrong, Layton thought. "There's plenty of time."

"The funeral is planned for Tuesday afternoon. That is, if the coroner . . ."

"I know," Layton said.

"Mr. Everglade said he expected to know definitely by tonight." She was still staring ahead. "Was there any special reason for your dropping by, Jim?"

"I guess I thought you might be lonely."

That made her look at him again. She said softly, "That was kind of you, Jim."

"I'm the kind kind," he said. "How did the rest of the press treat you today. Were they the kind kind, too?"

"You know how they were. They were horrible."

Neither spoke again until Layton drove into the funeral-home parking lot.

He helped her out, and she said quietly, "I'm sorry, Jim, but I always seem to offend you somehow. I wish I knew what I do or say that rubs you the wrong way."

"It's not you," Layton said, and he was appalled at the stiffness in his voice, "believe me, Nancy. I have . . . certain personal problems. It's not your fault at all. I'm sorry if I made you think it was."

"Oh," Nancy said. "Well. Thanks a lot, Jim, for driving me in." She extended a slim, gloved hand formally. "I don't want to waste any more of your evening. Good-by."

This time he managed to say, "Good-by nothing! I haven't a thing on for tonight. I'll drive you back."

"I wouldn't dream of letting you do that. I'll take a taxi."

"You won't do anything of the sort. I'll wait for you out here."

"Are you sure—?"

"I'm sure, Nancy."

She looked at him searchingly. Then she touched his arm and turned and walked toward the side entrance of the funeral home.

Layton stood watching her. For some reason a picture of the Beverly Hills carhop's wiggle flashed into his mind. That had been frank sexual insolence. Nancy's walk was without guile or challenge—the merest natural sway of the hips, just noticeable enough to make him turn abruptly away. It's like her perfume, he thought: it doesn't exist except for somebody very close . . .

That made him think of Tutter King.

She was even paler than usual when she came out. He held the car door open, not touching her this time, and shut it carefully and went around to slide under the wheel. As he turned on the ignition Layton said, "Bad?"

"I hated it!"

78

He was surprised by the passion in her voice. "Hated what, Nancy?"

"Picking out the casket, discussing prices, materials, arrangements . . . People shouldn't have to buy funerals like a case of beans in a supermarket?"

"I know what you mean." He released his brake and began to back out of the parking space, deliberately not looking at her. He had seen the tears starting in her eyes.

For Tutter King.

For a two-timing heel on whom she'd thrown away the best years of her life.

Layton drove out of the lot trying to shut his ears against the helpless sounds of her weeping. His gas gauge was hovering around the *E* and he was short of cash; I'd better stick around the neighborhood, he thought, until she stops crying and I can head into Joe's. He had a charge account at Joe's.

He drove slowly, making right turns. When out of the corner of his eye he saw her put a handkerchief to her nose, and then begin looking herself over in her compact mirror, he sighed with relief and made for the gas station.

"All I seem to do when you're around," Nancy said in a sniffly voice, "is imitate a waterfall. I'm sorry, Jim. I know men dislike weepy women."

"Not me," Layton said. "Nine out of every ten women in this town have forgotten how to cry. Uh-uh," he said, as if he had just noticed, "I'd better stop for gas."

She looked down at her lap as he pulled into the station. She kept looking down.

"Fill her up, Joe," Layton said.

"Hi, Mr. Layton." Joe stuck the nozzle of the gas hose into the old car's tank and left it on automatic. He got his squirt bottle and a length of paper toweling and came around to clean the windshield. Joe was a paunchy old-timer with skin like grilled toast. "Say, Mr. Layton, I meant to talk to you about your windshield. The glass is scraped almost clean through. Could be dangerous."

"It's because of the sap dripping from the trees in front of my apartment house," Layton said gloomily. "Hardens the wipers so they cut like steel. How much would a new windshield set me back, Joe?"

"I'll have to look it up. But it don't have to set you back nothing." Joe grinned through the glass he was cleaning. "You carry comprehensive, don't you?"

"Yes, but it doesn't cover things like this."

"It covers glass breakage, don't it? So just before you bring it into the shop, wham it. The insurance companies never question broken glass."

79

"Thanks, Joe." Layton grinned back. "But no, thank you. You know me. The original square."

Joe shook his head and went around to remove the hose, which had shut itself off. He hung it back on the pump, screwed the cap on the tank, returned to investigate the oil and water situation, and finally made out the charge slip. All the while he kept shaking his head. Layton watched him with amusement.

He handed Layton the pad and said grumpily, "Do I put a new windshield in or don't I?"

"Well . . . all right," Layton said. "When do you want the car, Joe?" He signed the slip and handed the pad back.

"Better make it Monday," Joe said, giving Layton the carbon. "I got a big week next week. I'll have Billy get the new shield early Monday morning. Monday okay?"

"I'll drop it off first thing."

As Layton started the car Joe, visibly struggling with his better judgment, turned back. "Look, Mr. Layton. I hate to see you have to shell out for a new shield when all you have to do is wham this one with a small sledge—I'll lend you one—"

"Joe, it isn't honest."

The garage man stared at him. "What do you mean it ain't honest? What are you, a millionaire or something? These insurance companies expect it. Everybody does it."

Not everybody, Joe." Layton smiled. "Thanks just the same."

"Beats me!" Joe said. "Well, I'll try to hold the cost down, Mr. Layton. Okay if I phone a few auto graveyards to see if I can locate a good used one?"

"Okay? I'll kiss you!" Layton waved and drove out.

He became uncomfortably aware as he drove north that Nancy was giving him quizzical sidelong glances. "I don't know whether you're an oddball, Jim, or just too good to be true. You meant that back there, didn't you?"

"Of course," Layton said shortly.

"I've been trying to think of a single person I know who wouldn't have taken Joe's advice, and I can't. Tutter would have tipped Joe five dollars and borrowed the hammer."

"Maybe that's why Tutter wound up taking payola," Layton retorted. Then he mumbled, "I'm sorry, Nancy. I shouldn't have said that."

She was silent. "Have you ever been offered a substantial —well, gift not to print something?" she asked suddenly.

Layton said, "Yes," and let it go at that.

"And didn't take it?"

"No."

"That was a bad example," Nancy murmured. "You

80

wouldn't be working for a newspaper reporter's salary if you didn't have respect for your job. But if you were offered a million dollars?"

"That's an even worse example," Layton said with a grin. "It's purely academic."

"But if you were? Would you turn it down, Jim?" There was a curious urgency in her tone that stirred him. She apparently felt a need to cut him down to her dead husband's size.

Layton thought a long time. "I don't suppose you'll believe me. Yes, I think I'd turn it down."

"A million dollars?" She didn't believe him. Or maybe, Layton thought, she didn't want to believe him.

"Look, Nancy," he said, "honesty is almost entirely a matter of training and precept. I'm the kind of shmo who was unlucky enough to have been brought up by parents who not only preached honesty, but lived it. The day I was twelve years old my father and mother took me to the movies for my birthday. Pop not only paid full fare for me on the bus, but when the cashier at the movies asked him how many, he promptly said, 'Three adult.' And I was a scrawny, undersized kid who could have passed for ten. . . . To this day I can't even pocket a public phone jackpot—you know, when instead of getting your dime back a whole handful of silver comes pouring out. I send it back to the phone company. You don't believe me, do you?" He glanced at her.

"You *are* unbelievable," she murmured. "What was your father, a minister?"

"Pop?" Layton chuckled. "He was a mail carrier."

They were well out into the Valley before Nancy spoke again. "I realize now why you despised Tutter."

"Tutter was only a symptom, Nancy. Our whole civilization is on the take. I suppose you could say I despise humanity."

"Oh, no, Jim!"

"Well"—Layton smiled—"maybe with an exception here and there."

"You mean your wife and children?" She was looking at the road.

"Wife and children?" He turned to stare at her. "I'm not married. Never could afford it."

"Oh," Nancy King said.

When he helped her out of his car at her door, she asked him in for a nightcap. But she looked so exhausted that Layton took her off the hook. "You'd better hit the sack, Nancy, before you fall on your face."

"I am tired," she murmured. "I think I'm going to be

81

able to sleep tonight. Somehow, our talk relaxed me. I'm so grateful, Jim. I feel as if I've known you for years."

He muttered, "Good night," and turned to the car.

"Jim."

"Yes, Nancy." He did not quite turn back.

"Will·I see you at the funeral?"

"If I'm assigned to cover it."

"I see."

She unlocked her door quickly and went inside. Layton jumped into his car and took off in a shower of gravel.

« 12 »

Layton was in the Police Building by 8:20 A.M. There were already half-a-dozen officers in the Homicide squad room. Detective Sergeants Harry Trimble and Ed Winterman were seated side·by side at one of the long tables; Winterman was filling out a form and Trimble seemed to be telling him what to write down.

As Layton strolled in, the hot-shot speaker coughed and began to blare: "Attention all units vicinity Vermont Avenue and Olympic Boulevard. ADW northeast corner intersection. Victim down, dead or seriously injured. Suspect armed with hatchet last seen proceeding on foot south on Vermont. Description WMA, dark complexion, black hair . . ."

Everyone in the squad room had automatically stopped to listen. At the "Approach with caution" sign-off one detective, with a Mexican face, hung up the phone he had been using. "Sandy and I'll take it. Let's roll, Sandy." A towheaded officer hurried out after him. The remaining officers, including Trimble and Winterman, just as automatically resumed what they had been doing. Layton had to remind himself that all over Greater Los Angeles people were either getting ready to go to church or turning luxuriously over in bed.

Trimble nodded at Layton's approach. Winterman did not even bother to raise his head.

"Park it, Layton," Trimble said. To his partner he said, "Can the report for now, Ed." Winterman slipped the form into a file folder sourly.

Layton sat down on the opposite side of the table. "Understand you were looking for me late yesterday. You come up with something?"

82

"A couple of pretty good motives for murder," Layton said.

The glass eye stared at him. "For instance."

Layton took the recording company Christmas letters to Hathaway from his breast pocket and tossed them across the table. Both detectives reached for them quickly. "Note that every one of these, at the bottom, refers to the enclosure of a check. There were lots more letters, but I only took the ones where the secretary had pulled the boner. Motive?"

"Could be," the one-eyed detective said. He seemed angry. "How'd you get these, Layton? From where?"

"George Hathaway's wife. She's suing him for a divorce."

"I know that." Trimble's anger, Layton suddenly realized, was directed at Winterman. It must have been Winterman's job to check out Hathaway. The swarthy sergeant's complexion was beginning to look like old mahogany. "I appreciate this, Layton."

"One thing, Sergeant," Layton said. "I promised to try to keep these letters out of the papers, with the single proviso that you don't charge Hathaway with murder and have to use them as evidence. How about it?"

Trimble did not hesitate. "If the D.A. will go along, so will we."

"Also, if the D.A. decides he has to release them, I want my exclusive. I'm not doing you guys' work for no pay, and on top of that letting myself be scooped on my own story."

"I'm sure the D.A.'ll agree to that." Trimble's scar writhed. "But you said something about a couple of motives, Layton."

"This one is privileged, so I can't tell you its source. It's a pip—a double-barreled pip." Winterman was hanging on every word, and Layton felt sorry for him. "Hubert Stander—"

"Stander?" the one-eyed detective said.

"Hubert Stander secretly owns a controlling interest in one of the big recording companies—Southwestern. He'd be in trouble if the FCC found out. He knew all about King's payola deals, and he turned his back in return for King's plugging Southwestern discs. So on that count alone Stander had at least as much reason to be scared of what King was going to 'announce' at the end of his last show as Hathaway had."

"And the other barrel?" Trimble asked. Winterman had slunk far down in his chair.

"Lola Arkwright used to bed down in a love nest Stander

83

was paying for. Tutter King came along and she switched beds."

"That one we knew," Winterman said quickly.

Trimble was drumming on the table. "The info about Stander and Southwestern is privileged, you say. You're not a lawyer, Layton. You can't plead privilege. Who was the source of your information?"

"Whoa, Napoleon, not so fast," Layton said. "Not only *can* reporters plead privilege, they do it all the time. And I'm doing it now."

Trimble said dryly, "A lot of judges have disagreed with your interpretation of the law, Counselor. And the reporters wound up in jail."

Layton held out his wrists. "Let's go, Sergeant."

Trimble grinned. "You're more valuable to me nosing around. I'm pretty damn sure I know who gave you the dope on Stander, anyway. Any more tidbits, Layton?"

"Well," Layton drawled, "old Hubert Stander is out of town. Did you give him permission to go?"

"Hell, no!" Trimble looked at Winterman, and Winterman shook his head with great vigor. "Where'd he go, do you know?"

"No. But a maid or housekeeper or something—name is Helga—told me he's due back by plane at eleven this morning."

"You're a one-man police force," Trimble growled. "Thanks, Layton. We'll be waiting for Mr. Stander on his exclusive patio. Anything else?"

"Yes. Now you can do something for me. What's Lola Arkwright's home address?"

Trimble sent Winterman a curt nod, and the squat detective got up like a good boy eager to please and went to a tier of filing cabinets.

"Pagoda Apartments, apartment sixteen," Winterman said, after searching through a manila folder. "That's in the nine-hundred block on Palm Street. North Hollywood."

Layton jotted down the address. "What's her phone number, Sergeant? She's not in the book."

Winterman gave him a number.

"Thanks, gentlemen." Layton put his notebook away and rose. "See you tomorrow morning at the inquest."

It was a one-story U-shaped pink stucco building with a veranda running around the front and sides, the door to each of its several dozen apartments opening onto the veranda. Palm Street was nearly at the Beverly Hills line. The Pagoda Apartments looked expensive.

Apartment 16 was in the left arm of the U.

It was a few minutes to ten when Layton pressed the doorbell. Faint chimes sounded. He waited ninety seconds and then pressed the bell button again.

He was about to ring it a third time when a door chain rattled and the door opened not quite as far as the chain would allow. Lola Arkwright's face peered out. Her eyes looked puffed and sleepy, her red hair was tousled, and he could dimly make out a negligee with a nightgown underneath.

"Oh, it's you," she said. Even her voice sounded mussed. "What do you want?"

"In," Layton said. "Palaver."

"For God's sake," she said. "You woke me up. Come back in an hour."

"My intentions are strictly reportorial." Layton smiled. "You can duck behind a screen or something while we talk."

"I don't have a screen. You'll have to come back."

"All right, Miss Arkwright." Layton shrugged. "I'll wait out here on the veranda."

"No," the redhead said sharply. "I don't want my neighbors seeing a man hanging around my door. Will you *please*—?"

Something clicked in Layton's head. This wasn't in character.

"Then let me wait inside," he said. "Unhook the chain. I'll give you a chance to make it back to the bedroom."

"Nothing doing!" Scared. What was she scared about? "If you don't go away right now I won't talk to you at all!"

"There you have me." Layton made it sound rueful. "Okay, honey, to wait in my car? At least that way you can signal me when you're dressed. Maybe it won't take you an hour."

He could feel the pressure behind her hesitation. Finally she said, "All right," in a sweet voice, and shut the door. Layton heard the click of the bolt.

As he sauntered past her windows on the veranda, he noticed out of the corner of his eye two slats of a Venetian blind part slightly. He grinned to himself and made for his car. He had parked almost at the end of the left side of the building, and he walked toward the car in a careless manner. When he got to the car he looked casually back, just in time to see the two slats close.

Immediately he made for the rear. There was an archway, as he had suspected, leading to a courtyard, into which opened rear exits from each apartment.

Layton settled himself in a deep shadow beside the archway, lit a cigarette, and waited.

He was working on his third cigarette when his wait was rewarded.

The rear door of apartment 16 opened and a tall man stepped hurriedly out. He was carrying a small overnight bag. He strode toward the archway as if he were late for an appointment, squinting in the strong sun. As he passed under the arch Layton caught a whiff of fresh after-shave lotion.

The man was expensively dressed and he had gray hair.

Layton stepped out of his shadow in the distinguished man's wake and tapped him lightly on the shoulder.

The man whirled as if he had been stabbed.

"Morning, Mr. Stander," Layton said cheerfully.

« 13 »

Stander made a remarkable recovery. Almost as he whirled and recognized his accoster the fear began to drain out of his face, to be replaced by calculation.

"Good reflexes, Mr. Stander," Layton said. "I'm kind of glad you're not carrying a weapon."

The steel eyes bored into him. "You're like the rest of your tribe, Layton. Peeping Toms, the lot of you. Where's your photographer?" He actually glanced around as if to spot a camera with a telephoto lens aimed at him from some distant vantage point.

"If I were after that kind of story," Layton said, "I'd have been in the bedroom of the apartment with a photographer fifteen minutes ago."

"Bedroom of what apartment? What are you talking about?"

"Now, now, Mr. Stander." Layton smiled. "This isn't worthy of you. I'm referring, as you very well know, to the bedroom of apartment sixteen. What you tell your wife and servants about where you spend your weekends is of no interest to me—except as it may have a bearing on Tutter King's murder."

"Murder." KZZX's chairman of the board reflected. "You use the word, Layton," he said slowly, "as if it were an established fact. Have the police decided it was murder?"

"I've decided it was murder, Mr. Stander." It was interesting to Layton that the tall man made no further attempt to play the innocent about his tryst.

"On what grounds?"

"On a number of grounds. The one that brought me here this morning is particularly interesting."

"And that is?"

"Your tie-up with Lola Arkwright."

Stander regarded him with great frankness. "I don't suppose it would do the slightest good to assure you that I dropped into Miss Arkwright's apartment this morning on a business matter—"

"Carrying an overnight bag, and sneaking out the back door smelling of just-applied after-shave lotion?" Layton shook his head gravely. "Not the slightest good."

"I thought not." Stander's tone was actually regretful. "Layton, how much do you know?"

"About you and Lola? Pretty much the whole story, Mr. Stander."

"Who told you?"

Layton shook his head.

"I take it, then, you consider that King, Lola, and I formed the usual triangle?"

"I don't consider it, Mr. Stander. I know it."

"As a result of which, I further take it, you believe I had a motive to kill King?"

"Didn't you?"

"Not a bit of it." Stander took Layton's arm and companionably walked him away from the entrance to the courtyard. "If you've dug up this much about me, Layton, you must also have found out the kind of background I come from, the social circle in which Mrs. Stander and I move?"

Layton nodded.

"Then you must know how little this Arkwright girl means to me."

"No dice, Mr. Stander," Layton said. "Tutter took her away from you. Here you are, less than forty-eight hours after his death, back in her bed. That doesn't sound to me like disinterest."

"I'm disappointed in you, Layton," the man of distinction said. "Of course I'm not disinterested. The girl is sexually attractive to me, and she's compliant. But if you think I'd commit murder over her, you're a very naïve young man. The Lolas in this town are a dime a dozen. I could have all the Lolas I want by snapping my fingers. She happens to be handy, that's all. I'll admit it was very foolish of me to take up with her again so soon after King died, especially under the circumstances. But I give you my word it was folly, nothing more sinister."

"Have you told Lola any of this?" Layton murmured.

Stander's expression lost its friendliness. He pointedly glanced at his watch.

"By the way, Mr. Stander," Layton went on, "the police know all about this, too."

The tall man's cold eyes flickered. He turned on his heel and began to walk away.

"Oh, before you go. There's one thing more."

Stander stopped in mid-stride. He turned around and came back.

"You're beginning to annoy me, Layton," he said. "What is it this time?"

"You had another good reason for wanting Tutter King out of the way. Especially before he could make that surprise announcement he'd promised for the end of his show."

Stander stood very still. "And what was that?"

"Your involvement in the payola mess. You had an understanding with King that you'd keep your mouth shut about his payola graft if he'd plug the discs of the Southwestern Recording Company, in which—under cover—you hold the controlling interest. You could hardly have been unaware that that might have been the little surprise good old Tutter had in mind for his swan song on KZZX."

The chairman of the board blinked quite rapidly. That's the killer, Layton thought—the one he didn't expect. Layton could almost hear the gears whirring and meshing under the gray hair. He could only admire the quiet way in which Stander asked, "Who told you that libelous story?"

"A reporter is like a prospector, Mr. Stander," Layton said. "He doesn't advertise where he's struck pay dirt. He just cashes in on it."

He was almost sorry he had put it that way; a flash of hope glittered for an instant in Stander's eyes. "Am I to take that, Layton, as a bid for a bribe?"

"It was an unfortunate figure of speech, Mr. Stander. Among my few assets is an itchless palm."

"Incorruptible, eh?" Stander sneered.

"The last honest man," Layton said, nodding.

Stander studied his tormentor for a long time. Then he said, in the same unnaturally quiet tone, "I don't think we have anything more to say to each other," and stalked away.

The millionaire's parting words had left an ominous echo behind.

As if it had been a declaration of war.

The front door to apartment 16 opened before Layton could take his finger from the bell button. Lola was dressed in a black skirt, a white blouse, and open-toed sandals that revealed immaculate little feet with toenails painted the exact red of her hair. She had carefully combed and brushed her hair and made up her face.

"I thought you were in such a hurry to talk to me," she said, stepping back. "I was ready five minutes ago and you didn't answer my signal."

Layton walked past her into a two-level living room. Everything in the room earned his respect, from the art on the walls to the wall-to-wall nylon carpeting on the floor. The furniture was exquisite. If the whole apartment was like this, the rent must be astronomical. With Tutter dead, it must have been a relief to Lola that Stander was willing to take her back, complete with monthly bills.

"You didn't say where you were," Lola said. She had shut the door and was standing flat against it, watching him.

"Out back," Layton said, "talking to Stander."

After a moment the redhead shrugged and strolled over to a divan and flung herself on it. She reached for a cigarette and a lighter. Layton took it from her and held the flame to the cigarette. She nodded and lay back, inhaling.

"You may as well park it, Fido," she said. "You're a tough hound to shake." She patted the divan.

Layton sat down in a nearby chair. "Well?"

"Well, what?"

"Don't you have anything to say?"

"Yes." She laughed. "I'd like to have seen Hubie's face."

"Hubie," Layton said. "And what does Hubie call you— Lollipop?"

"Something like that," Lola said lazily. "I thought you were working on the case."

"I am."

At that she sat up and flicked her ashes into a tray and pulled her skirt down over her knees. "I don't think that's funny, McGee. What's the angle?"

"The angle is this," Layton said patiently. "I think Tutter was murdered. Tutter took you away from Stander. Tutter dies with an ice pick in his heart. Before he can be buried Stander spends the night with you."

She crushed her butt out with slow, remorseless pressure. "That smells, do you know that?"

"I can't help its odor. I've just strung a few facts together. How do they stack up to you?"

She sank back against the wall and regarded him quite steadily. "Stupid," she said. "Do you honestly think any man would commit murder over me?"

"Do you honestly expect me to believe you mean that?"

"You're damn tootin' I mean it, Layton," the redhead said. "Sure, I attract men. I'm the girl of their dreams—their sex dreams. But somehow there's never a wedding ring mixed up in it."

"I thought Tutter wanted to marry you."

Her lips twisted. "So did I. But I was kidding myself. I realize now that he conned me into thinking of myself as a bride on the basis of a few vague promises that didn't add up to a thing. How in hell could he marry me when all along he was living with his wife and enjoying every minute of it?" She grabbed for another cigarette and Layton lit it for her. She began to smoke in quick, bitter spurts.

"So you've come around to believing that Nancy King was telling the truth."

"Yes. The police checked her out. Can you imagine that bastard playing me that way—and me falling for it?"

Layton said nothing.

"Maybe I was lucky at that. If I'd found out beforehand what a sucker he was playing me for, I might have been tempted to go after him with an ice pick myself. As it is"—she shrugged again—"it's left me free to hop right into bed with somebody else."

"With an old man?"

"Hubie?" Lola showed her white teeth. "He's not so old where it counts. And these old bucks can be mighty grateful to a girl for making them feel twenty-one again. He's been very generous to me."

"I take it you and Stander got together again on his initiative, not yours?"

"Yes, Mr. Layton," Lola Arkwright said icily. "I don't call men, they call me. When the day comes that I have to do the calling, you'll find that I took an accidental overdose of sleeping pills."

"It sort of surprised me," Layton murmured, "that he'd risk going back to you so soon after King's death."

That seemed to please her. "Hubie's always had a big thing for me. He never really gave up after I left him for Tutter. I had to keep saying no."

"And you don't think he might have killed King to change your no back to a yes?"

"Men don't kill for the likes of me. I told you."

"What's the matter with the likes of you? You're attractive, you have brains—"

The redhead laughed. "Don't tell me you're on the make, too." She shook her head. "In Hubie's book I'm an occasional night's fun. In my book he's the guy who pays my bills. That's all it ever was and all it ever will be."

90

"Well, the stories jibe," Layton said. "That's about what Stander told me, too."

"What do you mean?" Lola said. "What did Stander tell you?"

"He ridiculed the idea that he would commit murder over you," Layton said; he had to keep his voice flat and dehumanized to be able to say it at all. "I think I can quote him verbatim: 'The Lolas in this town are a dime a dozen. I could have all the Lolas I want by snapping my fingers. She happens to be handy, that's all.' "

She jumped off the divan as if he had slapped her. She stood over Layton, white-faced, with clenched hands.

"Hubie said that? To you?"

"Yes, Lola," Layton said.

"You're lying in your teeth!"

"Didn't you just tell me practically the same thing?"

She was shaking in her fury. "The—!" she said thickly. "A dime a dozen, am I? That's going to cost him a hell of a lot more than a dime! He'll be crawling on his belly—without that corset he wears!—before I'm through with him!"

Layton sat quietly.

She stopped shaking and sat down suddenly. "Maybe Stander did kill Tutter. Tutter had something on him."

"What?" Layton asked.

"I don't know exactly. But after he was fired Tutter told me he could pull Hubie down with him if he wanted to—and George Hathaway, too, come to think of it."

"They were in on the payola?" He wondered how much she knew.

She looked at him then, as if she had forgotten he was there.

"I talk too much," Lola Arkwright said. "So maybe Hubie did stick that thing into Tut. That leaves Tutter with his toes turned up and Hubie still able to write checks. He sure as hell wouldn't be able to after a visit to the gas chamber. Nice to have seen you, Mr. Layton."

Layton got up and went out.

« 14 »

It was after eleven when Layton drove away from the Pagoda Apartments. Turning west on Sunset, he turned off at Lomitas and headed for Crescent Drive.

Hubert Stander's house was a mammoth three story of

elderly vintage surrounded by elderly eucalyptus trees and elderly box hedges. To one side of the vast lawn glimmered a swimming pool of an outmoded type beside which a stout woman sat sunning herself.

There were no cars either in the driveway or at the curb. Since the two Homicide men had not yet arrived, Layton drove past without hesitation. On Santa Monica Boulevard he found a cheap restaurant and had an early lunch.

It was almost noon when he returned to the Crescent Drive house. This time a shiny Ford sedan was standing at the curb, and two men with their hats in their hands were talking to the woman in the lawn chair. Layton spotted Sergeant Trimble's scar. He parked behind the Ford and crossed the lawn to the pool.

The detectives glanced around at his approach.

Trimble said, "I thought you'd turn up. You work all day Sunday, too?"

Layton smiled. "That makes three of us."

Winterman ignored him.

The woman was about fifty, Layton judged, a fifty gone to blubber and pot. She had a fat, bland, pleasant face framed by dull dark hair turning dirty gray. Her stout figure was encased in a modest blue sun suit through which he could see the ribs of an old-fashioned corset. Her shapeless bare legs were lumpy skinned, with an intricate network of varicose veins that made them look like old maps.

"Jim Layton, Mrs. Hubert Stander," Trimble said. "Layton's from the *Bulletin*."

"How do you do, Mr. Layton. My goodness! Police officers, now a reporter. What on earth is this all about?"

"Tutter King," the one-eyed detective said.

"How silly of me not to have guessed," Mrs. Stander exclaimed. "Hubert's one of your witnesses, isn't he? So sad, such a young man committing suicide."

There was an air of good-natured vagueness about her, as though she were constantly peering at things she did not quite understand but was ready to take on faith.

Trimble said, "You say, Mrs. Stander, that your husband flew to Las Vegas yesterday evening. Do you happen to know why?"

"I believe Hubert mentioned that it was at Mr. Hathaway's request. Some act or other they're considering putting on at KZZX. Hubert enjoys talent scouting, and Mr. Hathaway often asks him to take such trips."

So that was how Hathaway knew of Stander's extramarital activities, Layton thought. He was Stander's regular alibi.

"But why do you want to see my husband?" the stout

woman asked. "I thought Hubert had answered all your questions."

Ed Winterman said, "There's a couple more we thought of."

She looked puzzled. "Well, he ought to be home any minute now."

"Oh, Mrs. Stander," Layton said, "did you happen to be watching The King's Session with Mr. Stander Friday?"

"No, I missed it," she said sadly. "I always miss everything exciting. Mr. Stander watched it alone."

Layton caught Trimble's good eye, and Trimble nodded for him to keep going. "I suppose he always watched the show."

"Heavens, no, Mr. Layton. Hubert isn't interested in such childish things as dance music. He watched Tutter King's show Friday because he was afraid the young man might make some tactless remark over the air—being fired, you know, his last show, and so on. As it turned out, Hubert had good reason to feel apprehensive."

"That announcement King made at the beginning, huh?" Sergeant Trimble asked casually.

"Yes. Hubert was terribly disturbed. He kept walking around the house and looking at his watch—poor dear, he didn't know *what* that young man was going to say. Finally —oh, it must have been twenty minutes to four or so—I heard him go into the kitchen and start rummaging around, banging cupboard drawers—I've *never* known Hubert to be so upset—and when I went into the kitchen and asked him what he was looking for, he shook his head and said he'd just found it—whatever it was—and he had to get over to the station. And he took the car and left."

"Drawers in the kitchen," Sergeant Winterman said. "I'd never have said Mr. Stander was the poke-around-in-the-kitchen type, would you, Harry?"

Trimble chuckled. Mrs. Stander looked doubtful, as if she were not quite sure where the humor lay. Layton glanced at Trimble, and he felt a sudden chill.

The one-eyed detective took a huge handkerchief out of his pocket and swabbed the back of his neck. "Say, Mrs. Stander, while we're waiting for your husband, would you mind if I went up the house and got a glass of water? Talking about kitchens reminded me."

"How thoughtless of me," Mrs. Stander said. She began to struggle to her feet. "I'll go right in and make you some mint juleps."

"I wouldn't think of disturbing you," Sergeant Trimble said firmly. "You sit right back down there, Mrs. Stander! What's your maid's name again?"

"Helga?" Mrs. Stander giggled. "Oh, dear, don't let Helga hear you call her a maid. She runs *everything!* I'm just a parasite."

"I guess she must be in the kitchen getting dinner," Winterman remarked.

"Oh, yes. On Sundays we eat promptly at one. You're sure you don't want me to make you some juleps?"

"We're not allowed to drink on duty, Mrs. Stander," Trimble said. "You're thirsty, Ed, aren't you?"

"Yeah," Winterman said.

"Excuse me, Mrs. Stander," Layton said. "I think I'd like some water, too."

"Oh, dear," the stout woman said again; but she sank back.

At the rear of the house there was a broad concrete apron separating the garage—it looked as if it might have been converted from an old carriage house—from the back porch. Trimble, Winterman, and Layton trudged up onto the porch and Trimble rapped on the screen door.

"Yah, yah?" A fat and buxom blond woman of Mrs. Stander's age, in a spotless white housedress was perched at a kitchen table deftly chopping raw cabbage with a big chef's knife. She did not look up until they had filed into the kitchen and the screen door banged. Then she inspected them briefly and returned her attention to the cabbage. "What is?"

"Police," Trimble said. The woman dropped the knife as if it had sliced off her finger. He flipped open his wallet and showed her his badge. Layton thought she was going to topple from the stool.

"I . . . do something?" she asked faintly.

"You're Helga what?"

"Helga Braunschweiger. I got already my first papers—"

"Relax, Helga," Trimble said. "We just want some information. Do you have an ice pick?"

"Ice pick?" Her thick lips remained parted. "Yah?"

The two detectives exchanged glances.

"We'd like to see it."

"Ice pick, ice pick," Helga said, raising her leviathan bottom from the stool and looking around in a panic. "Where do I see the ice pick?" She trundled over to the cabinets and began pulling drawers open. "I got to think where is it. Today everything is freezers with ice cubes . . ."

"Here, lemme help you look," Sergeant Winterman said.

"Wait!" Helga panted triumphantly. "I remember. In this one I see it. Yah." She pulled a drawer open. It was a mess of small tools and miscellaneous hardware items. "Ach, that Mr. Stander! A thousand times I tell him from my kitchen to stay out . . ." She glanced up at the men with a frightened look. "It is not here now. Mister Policemen, with my own hands I put it here—"

"When?" Trimble said. Winterman was going through the drawer like a petty thief on the run. He shook his head at Trimble and went to work on the other drawers.

"Long, long time. For what do I need an ice pick? In here I put it so I do not stick myself—"

"When did you see it last, Helga?"

The woman moaned. "When . . . when . . . ?" She looked up eagerly. "Now I remember! What today is?—Sunday . . . Saturday, Friday, Thursday—three days ago I see it! In the drawer, Mister Policeman. The drawer I open a thumbtack to get, and almost I stick myself on the *verdammte* ice pick—it is so sharp, the point—"

"Yeah," Sergeant Trimble said. "That's fine, Helga. You're going great. Now tell me: What did that ice pick look like? Describe it."

"Was here when I come work for Mrs. Stander. Four years already. But like new. Like never used it was."

"But what did it look like? The handle, for instance?"

"Like? Like wood, plain wood. No paint. But with varnish over."

"No ice pick, Harry," Ed Winterman said. Every drawer in the kitchen was open, the contents a hopeless jumble.

"Thanks, Helga," the one-eyed detective said, and he nodded curtly at his partner. "Let's go."

"What's going on here?" a voice demanded.

Hubert Stander, carrying the small overnight bag, was glaring through the screen door.

"You better come in, Mr. Stander," Trimble said slowly. "We have some talking to do."

The chairman of the board of Station KZZX seated himself carefully in the fine old morocco-leather wing chair behind the hand-carved walnut desk. He had led them in silence through a spacious living room filled with what Layton suspected were show pieces of antique furniture to the tall, walnut-paneled, book-lined study.

Layton gently shut the door. Mrs. Stander was still sunning herself on the lawn. He could see her through the narrow opening in the brown velvet drapes.

Under other circumstances Layton would have quailed under Stander's pale, contemptuous glance. "I suppose," the distinguished-looking man said to the two detectives, "this Peeping Tom of a so-called newspaperman had told you all about Lola and me."

"Why, no, Mr. Stander," Sergeant Trimble said, and Stander's pallor deepened. "What's all this, Layton?"

"I didn't get a chance to tell you," Layton said. "Thanks, Mr. Stander, for doing it for me. Stander wasn't in Las Vegas last night, Sergeant, and the only talent he was scouting was in Lola Arkwright's apartment. He spent the night there."

"And I was going to throw the book at you for leaving town without permission," Trimble said to Stander.

"Well, I didn't," Stander said through compressed lips. "And since I didn't, I can't see that where I spent the night is anyone's concern but mine."

"You can't?" Trimble said. There was the thinnest edge of triumph to his voice. "It just about rounds out one of your two possible motives for killing King."

Stander placed his large, square hands flat on his desk. "I've already discussed both of them with Layton. It's absurd for you or anyone else to think that either would make me take a human life. Anyway, motives hardly constitute evidence. Is there anything else, Sergeant?"

"Yes," Trimble said. "Where's the ice pick that was in your kitchen tool drawer as recently as the day before King was found with one just like it in his heart?"

"Ice pick?" Hubert Stander repeated. He licked his lips. "What are you talking about?"

"I'll spell it out for you, Mr. Stander. Your wife says you watched King's last show Friday—at least the start of it. She says King's announcement that he was going to make an important statement at the end of the show disturbed you enough for her to notice it—and I don't get the feeling that Mrs. Stander usually notices very much. She heard you opening drawers in the kitchen, looking for something. When she asked you what you were looking for you told her you'd found it, and you then left—in a hurry—for the TV station. According to your housekeeper, the tool drawer in the kitchen contained an ice pick which fits the description of the one that killed King. The ice pick is gone. Produce that ice pick, Mr. Stander, and we'll leave you to enjoy that delicious dinner I smell cooking."

Stander's pallor by now was alarming. He was making an undisguisable effort to control himself. "I don't know anything about an ice pick, Sergeant. I didn't even know we had one. And I haven't looked into the tool drawer in the kitchen for months. Small repair jobs around the house have always been done by our houseman or other servants."

"Give me their names," Sergeant Winterman said, pulling out a notebook.

"Right now we have no one but Helga." A slight beading

of sweat became visible on Stander's forehead. "Mrs. Stander has trouble keeping help. You see—"

Winterman put his notebook away, and Stander stopped. Trimble was getting colder and grimmer by the second. "You say you haven't looked into the tool drawer in the kitchen for months. Yet your wife told us she heard you opening drawers like mad in there. How is it you missed the tool drawer?"

"I . . . don't remember opening it. Maybe I did. If I did, I didn't see an ice pick—"

"Just what were you looking for in those drawers Friday afternoon, Mr. Stander?"

Stander said quickly, "My car keys. I thought I'd dropped them on the kitchen table on my way through before lunch. When I couldn't find them on the table I assumed Helga had put them away in a drawer. I opened most of the drawers looking for the keys until I suddenly remembered I hadn't put them on the table at all, I'd slipped them into my trousers pocket. And that's where I found them." There was a silence. The beads were now fat drops, one by one coursing down Stander's nose. "Don't you believe me, Sergeant? It's the truth!"

"I'm afraid, Mr. Stander," Trimble said, "I'm going to have to ask you to come downtown with us."

The man of distinction was beginning to take on a wild look. "You can't mean that. My wife . . . King committed suicide . . . You have no authority to arrest me in Beverly Hills—"

"Who said anything about arrest, Mr. Stander?" the one-eyed sergeant said. "I'm just asking you to accompany us downtown for further questioning."

"I won't go!"

"Ed," Trimble said to Winterman, "you'd better phone the Beverly Hills station and ask for a couple of their boys, pronto."

"Wait." And now Hubert Stander, chairman of the board of KZZX, was nakedly trembling. "I don't want a police car to be seen here . . . and don't tell my wife . . . I'll go with you."

"I think that's the sensible thing to do, Mr. Stander," Trimble said pleasantly.

Stander rose. "There's just one thing," he said in a very thick voice.

"What's that?"

"I want to phone my lawyer."

Sergeant Trimble made a gracious gesture toward the telephone on Stander's desk.

"Be my guest."

Layton anticipated the next few hours. They were bound to end in anticlimax, and they did.

He had no illusions about being allowed to sit in on the proceedings. The lawyer Stander had called said he would be waiting at the Police Building for them. No lawyer in his right mind would sanction the presence of a reporter under the circumstances, and Stander's lawyer came from the élite of Los Angeles' formidable array of legal talent. So Layton merely paused to watch Hubert Stander stoop over fat Mrs. Stander on the lawn and improvise a plausible fiction to explain his dinnerless departure with Trimble and Winterman; and when the tall gray man got into the rear of the shiny Ford with Trimble at his side and Winterman at the wheel, and was driven off—affectionately waving to his bewildered wife—Layton drove home.

He called the *Bulletin* and dictated his story. The city desk promised to send a man down to the Police Building for the follow-up, and Layton hung up to face what was left of his Sunday.

It was still early, and there were any number of things he could do. He could drive out to the beach; he enjoyed swimming, and he rarely got a chance to lie in the sun with nothing but trunks on. He could take in a movie; he liked movies. He could get on the phone and start working on the names in his little black book—names like Penny and Love and Alys and Marylouann (who insisted on having it spelled that way, and possessed other unusual ideas). He could—this never failed—call some of the boys and make up a poker game.

Instead, Layton stretched out on his couch with *Tropic of Cancer* and in the middle of a dirty word fell asleep.

His first thought when he woke up was: I'll call Nancy. He was actually reaching for the phone when he realized that he had intended to call her all along, and that he didn't know her number.

He was almost relieved at his ignorance. Lay off, Layton, lay off, he said to himself sternly; and he flung the paperback across the room, got off the couch, and went into the bathroom and plunged his head into a bowlful of cold water.

All through his solitary dinner he knew what he was going

to do. He was going to drive out into San Fernando Valley. He was going to find an excuse for doing so. He found the excuse, brushed the napkin across his mouth, grabbed his check, half ran to the cashier's desk, and then dived for the directory beside the phone booth.

Unlisted.

A colorful curse at the still-unburied corpse of Tutter King exploded in his head. Layton went into the booth and dialed the Homicide Division and asked for Lieutenant Jackson.

"Do me a favor, Lieutenant. I have to phone Tutter King's widow, and she's unlisted. I didn't think to note her number when I was out there. It's in the file."

"Seeing as how you're a privileged character around here," Jackson said, "hang on."

"Thanks," Layton said after noting the number. "By the way, what happened with Stander?"

"A big nothing," the lieutenant said.

"Figured," Layton said, grinning into the mouthpiece. "D.A. doesn't want a habeas slapped on Stander. A writ would force him to bring charges now. Tomorrow the coroner's jury sits—and who knows what their verdict will be? So the D.A. and Stander's lawyer make a deal—"

"Yeah, the lawyer promised to take personal responsibility and Stander was released in his custody without even having to put up bond." Jackson grunted. "What did you ask me for if you knew?"

"I didn't," Layton chuckled. "But Sunday is the D.A.'s day for golf." And he hung up.

He stared at his notation of Nancy King's telephone number for some time. Once he started to leave the booth. Finally, he dialed the number. When her voice sounded in his ear it went through him like the touch of a live wire. He almost hung up without responding.

But he did not. "Jim Layton," he said. "Hello again."

"Hello, Jim." She sounded pleased.

"You sound pleased," Layton said.

"I am."

"At what?"

"At your calling, silly."

"I'm pleased you're pleased."

She laughed. "I'm pleased you're pleased I'm pleased." He laughed.

Silence.

This is impossible, Layton thought desperately.

"Jim?"

"Yes, Nancy," he mumbled.

"Was that all you called to say?"

Layton inhaled. "No. How about my picking you up to-morrow morning and driving us down to the inquest togeth-er?"

She was silent again. But then she said, "No, Jim."

"Why not?" Layton heard himself demanding.

"Well . . . I can drive myself now, and I don't see why you should have to go all that extra distance—"

"You think it's because of my job, don't you?"

"Because of your job?" She seemed genuinely baffled.

"I'm a reporter," he said. "I've had the inside track on this story from the start. So naturally you'd think—"

Her quiet voice said, "Jim, that never crossed my mind."

"It didn't?"

"No. I don't think of you as a reporter after a story. I don't know why, but I never have."

A singing began in Layton's ears. "Then how about it?"

"How about what, Jim?"

"My driving you in the morning?"

Once more she was silent. Then suddenly he heard a vexed laugh. "We're both not very bright, are we? We for-got you won't have a car tomorrow. You're supposed to take it to your garage for a new windshield, remember?"

"Damn the new windshield!"

"No, Jim. I'll see you at the Hall of Justice."

Layton said, "I guess I'd better say good night, Nancy."

"Good night, Jim." Her voice was very soft. "And . . . thanks for thinking of me."

When he got home Layton kicked the Miller book back to the other side of the room and went to bed. He lay staring up into the darkness, hands clasped behind his head, for a timeless interval. He could not have said that he was think-ing, or even that he was feeling. All he was conscious of was the soft voice in endless repetition pronouncing his name.

Oddly, Layton overslept. By the time he had dropped his car off at Joe's and taxied down to the Hall of Justice, Cor-oner's Court was full.

In the second row of the section reserved for witnesses Layton saw Lola Arkwright, George Hathaway, Hubert Stander, and Nancy King. The two men were seated togeth-er between the two women. Stander had been careful not to sit next to Lola; he was between Hathaway and Nancy. All four were staring straight ahead.

There was no sign of Wayne Mission and Nora Perkins, even in the jammed spectator section. The district attor-ney's office must have decided for reasons of prudence to keep the proceedings entirely free of Tutter King's hysterical teenage admirers; there was not a youngster to be seen in the courtroom. Apparently Mrs. Stander and Linda Norman Hathaway were not present, either. Nor could Layton see Hazel Grant.

The two crime-lab men who had examined the KZZX dressing rooms on Friday were seated in the front row. With them was a thin, bald, keen-eyed man Layton recognized as some official from the coroner's office.

Harry Trimble was standing near the coroner's bench talking to a tired-looking young man with a brief case. Layton walked over.

"Hi," Trimble said. "This is Jim Layton, Artie. Arthur Cabot of the D.A.'s office."

They shook hands; Cabot's handshake was limp. "The reporter who found the body," he said, more as if he were checking off a mental item.

"That's right," Layton said. "Where do I sit—in the press section or with the witnesses?"

"Another problem!" the young assistant district attorney muttered. "The witnesses, the witnesses."

"The witnesses it is," Layton said; and he walked over to the second row and sat down beside Nancy. She kept staring ahead, but his arm was touching hers and he could feel her trembling. He was obscurely glad that she had not done the usual Hollywood bit and dressed in dramatic black *cum* widow's veil. She was wearing a simple dark gray suit and a gray silk blouse; her hat was an unassuming little cap of black felt.

The others did not acknowledge Layton's arrival, either. He sat back and folded his arms.

When the coroner—a tall, gaunt man with a shock of unruly black hair who looked remarkably like a clean-shaven Abraham Lincoln—entered the courtroom and took his place at the bench, Sergeant Trimble joined the row of witnesses, seating himself beside Lola Arkwright.

Trimble had hardly had time to warm the seat when he was called as the first witness.

He gave his name and rank, and immediately plunged into a factual account of his and Sergeant Winterman's investigation, beginning with the exact time of Layton's call to Homicide and their arrival at KZZX.

When the one-eyed detective had finished, the coroner said, "Sergeant, what conclusion did you draw concerning the probable manner in which the deceased died?"

"We listed it tentatively on the five point ten," Trimble replied, "as suspected suicide."

"The five point ten, so-called, is the investigating officer's report, Sergeant?"

101

"Yes, sir."

The coroner grasped the loose skin of his skinny neck between thumb and forefinger, and pulled—a nasty habit, Layton thought, for a man bearing the responsibility of a resemblance to Abraham Lincoln. "Does this mean that you discounted the possibility of murder?"

"No, sir."

"Would you develop that, Sergeant?"

Trimble explained in detail the physical layout of the area of KZZX in which King had been found dead, and he sketched in briefly the circumstances surrounding King's last telecast. "They were such," he went on, "as to open up the possibility that the deceased had been murdered. We found that *if* it was murder, only a few people had the opportunity to commit it." He named George Hathaway, manager of KZZX; Hubert Stander, chairman of the TV station's board; Lola Arkwright, deceased's assistant; Mrs. Nancy King, deceased's widow (here a murmur rippled through the room as hundreds of eyes focused upon Nancy, but she gave no sign that she was aware of them—no sign except to Layton, who felt her body quiver); and James Layton, newspaper reporter.

"There were also two teenage fans of Tutter King's who theoretically had opportunity," Trimble concluded, "but at no time were they out of each other's sight and they alibi each other. There is no reason of any kind to suppose that these minors had anything to do with King's death. I will name them if ordered to do so, but in a public hearing—"

"Right, quite right, Sergeant," the coroner said hastily. "You wish to ask a question, Mr. Cabot?"

The tired-looking young assistant district attorney said to Trimble, "How were you able to reduce the number of possible suspects—if this was murder—to so few persons, Sergeant? Weren't there several hundred people in the building at the time?"

Trimble went into an explanation in depth. When he had finished, the coroner asked, "Of the persons you have named who had opportunity, assuming this might have been homicide, Sergeant Trimble, were you able to pinpoint any with motive?"

"Yes, sir. Mr. George Hathaway and Mr. Hubert Stander."

A buzz began to swell, and the coroner admonished the spectators. Hathaway and Stander were so rigid that Layton had the ridiculous feeling that both men had stopped breathing.

"Develop that, Sergeant."

"Yes, sir. At the start of the telecast King announced

that he was going to make an important statement at the end of the show. He repeated this announcement before going off the air for the news-break intermission at 4 P.M., just a few minutes before he died. No one knows, or professes to know, what King meant to say, but there's plenty of testimony to the effect that he was very angry and bitter at both Mr. Hathaway and Mr. Stander for the cancellation of his show. We can't state it as a fact, but there's a strong possibility that what King intended to say at the end of the show concerned Mr. Hathaway or Mr. Stander, or both. We further established that Mr. Hathaway heard King's promise of a 'surprise announcement' on his office monitor, and that Mr. Stander heard it on his set at home."

Arthur Cabot asked, "Do you mean, Sergeant, that what King was in a position to reveal about Mr. Hathaway and/or Mr. Stander might have constituted a motive for murder in each case?"

"Possibly."

"In other words, Sergeant, public disclosure would have discredited or damaged the persons you have just named?"

"Yes, sir." Trimble added quickly, "But in Mr. Hathaway's case we discovered that he had instructed his chief control engineer, during the intermission, to cut King off the air if he began to say anything derogatory about anyone connected with KZZX. This would have shut King's mouth before he could damage Mr. Hathaway publicly, if that was what King meant to do. To that extent Mr. Hathaway had no immediate motive."

Hathaway was perspiring. Layton saw him begin to reach for a handkerchief, then stop.

The coroner leaned forward. "I remind the jury that no one is on trial here and that your sole duty is to determine the cause of death. While the coroner's jury has a choice of verdicts—homicide, justifiable homicide, suicide, accidental death, or death from natural causes—you are not empowered to elaborate on any of these possible verdicts by finding, for example, that death was by homicide at the hands of a specified person or persons. Even if the testimony should point to some individual as a murderer, the name of such individual cannot be included in the verdict. We are here today to get at the cause of Tutter King's death, and nothing more."

The coroner turned to Trimble. "Consequently, Sergeant, as you know, we have a great deal of latitude in these proceedings. In your opinion, is it necessary for the jury to know precisely what information the deceased had about Mr. Hathaway?"

"In my opinion, no, sir," the one-eyed detective said.

Layton heard Hathaway expel a long, tremulous breath. "It was nothing technically illegal, but to have it made public might cost Mr. Hathaway his job. I personally don't see that anything would be gained, for purposes of this proceeding, by putting it on the record."

"Can you tell us, Sergeant," the assistant district attorney asked wearily, "what information the deceased had in respect to Mr. Stander?"

Out of the corner of his eye Layton saw Stander stiffen.

"Yes, sir, because I have reason to believe it's going to be all over the newspapers soon, anyway. Mr. Stander secretly owns a substantial interest in a recording company. Under FCC regulations this constitutes a conflict of interest, since Mr. Stander is also chairman of the board of KZZX. However, Mr. Cabot, we discussed this with your office, and the consensus of legal opinion was that the only thing the FCC would do in such a case is insist that Mr. Stander dispose of his stock either in KZZX or in the recording company. Both stocks have gone up in value recently, so while to dispose of either holding might inconvenience Mr. Stander, he would certainly suffer no financial loss and would, in fact, gain."

"In short, then, Sergeant," Cabot said, "your considered opinion, as the police officer in charge of the investigation into King's death, and after discussing all aspects of the case with the district attorney's office, is that while various persons had the opportunity to murder the deceased, none possessed what you regard as a compelling motive? Is that a fair statement of your opinion?"

"Yes, sir."

Cabot glanced at the bench. The coroner nodded. "You may step down, Sergeant."

Layton was astounded. Trimble had not testified as to the ice pick missing from Hubert Stander's kitchen, or to any of Mrs. Stander's revelations. And he had not even hinted at the rivalry between Stander and King over Lola Arkwright's affections.

But on reflection Layton realized what must have happened. The police, the coroner's office, and the district attorney's office had agreed in advance that there was no evidence sufficient to warrant an indictment for murder.

Such prior agreement among the three agencies of the law was, of course, perfectly ethical. The thing that bothered Layton was that the agreement indicated fresh developments in the case of which he was totally ignorant.

« 16 »

The thin, bald, keen-eyed man seated in the front row was called to the stand and identified himself as Dr. Maxwell Swart, chief of the medical division of the coroner's office. Stripped of its medical terminology, Dr. Swart's testimony peeled down to what Layton already knew: the blade of an ice pick had penetrated the deceased's heart, causing immediate death; the angle of the wound was such that it could have been self-inflicted; there were no bruises, contusions, or other wounds on the body that might have indicated a struggle.

The police lab man, Lewis Mason, described his and his coworker's findings in room 1, where the body had been discovered, and in room 2, the disc jockey's dressing room. There had been no detectable sign of a struggle in either room. There had been no clues, of any nature, to indicate the presence of a second person in room 1 with the deceased, and no indication that King might have suffered the fatal stab-wound in room 2 and been dragged across the corridor to room 1. Shown a tagged ice pick by Cabot, Mason identified it as the ice pick he had found imbedded in King's chest.

"Were you able to trace this ice pick, Mr. Mason?"

"No, sir. It's of a very common type, sold by the thousands all over the country."

"Did you find fingerprints on the ice pick?"

"Yes, sir. Four, which we identified as coming from the right hand of the deceased."

"Which four, Mr. Mason?"

"All but the thumb."

"Were you able to establish whether deceased was right-handed or left-handed?"

"He was right-handed. Millions of TV viewers can testify to that from having watched him perform on his show for five years. We have affidavits to the same effect from numerous persons connected with Station KZZX who were in daily contact with him, and from Mrs. King."

"Was the position of deceased's four fingerprints on the ice pick handle compatible with, let us say, his having grasped the ice pick firmly to stab himself?"

"Yes, sir. The thumbprint was not laid down, of course,

105

because in grasping the handle the thumb would overlap the fingers."

"One thing more, Mr. Mason," young Cabot murmured. "Was there any indication on the ice pick, identifiable or not, of a print or prints *not* belonging to the deceased?"

"No, sir."

The photographer took the witness chair. He identified the photographs he had snapped of King's body and of the two dressing rooms. Prints of these photographs were handed around to the jury.

Layton was called. Prepared as he was for the predetermined course of the inquest, he was nevertheless surprised at the brevity of his questioning. Before he had time to adjust to the witness chair, it seemed to him, he was told to step down.

Hathaway, Stander, and Lola Arkwright received equally perfunctory treatment. Like Layton, they were merely asked to describe what they had done and seen during the news-break interval. In the redhead's case, Cabot asked two further questions.

"As Mr. King's assistant, Miss Arkwright," the young man from the D.A.'s office said, "you were very close to him from the time he reached the station on the day of his death, not to mention at other times?" Was there the faintest sardonic note in Cabot's murmur? Layton saw Lola flush; she had caught it, too. And he heard Nancy's almost inaudible sniff of contempt.

"Yes," Lola said defiantly.

"Did you notice anything strange in Mr. King's conduct that day?"

"Yes. He was nervous and jumpy. He put on a good act for other people, but he couldn't fool me."

"Nervous and jumpy," Cabot said. "That's all, Miss Arkwright."

He called Nancy King. After asking her the same preliminary questions about her movements during the newscast, he said, "Mrs. King, how did your husband take the cancellation of his TV contract by Station KZZX?"

"He was very upset," Nancy said in a low voice. "It meant that he was through on the air—at least, he thought it did."

"Would you describe his mental condition as depressed?"

She took a moment to think. "Bitter would be a better description. Bitter and angry."

The coroner interrupted. "You undoubtedly knew your husband better than anyone else, Mrs. King. Would you say he was high-strung, temperamental, given to sudden changes of mood?"

"Not any more than you'd expect from a popular performer. He had to be onstage a lot, as they say in show business, and that kind of life can be wearing." Nancy's glance went for a flick of time to the second row of the witness section. "But I would definitely not call my husband nervous and jumpy. At most times he was easy-going and good-natured."

The redhead's thin lips became thinner. Layton was furious. He could only imagine what the silent battle Nancy was compelled to wage in public with the woman she despised was costing her.

"Mrs. King," the coroner said, a little testily, "did your husband ever threaten to commit suicide?"

"Never," Nancy said firmly.

"Not even when he thought his career was finished?"

"No, sir. I still can't believe my husband took his own life. He had too much to live for, career or no career."

"Then it's your opinion, Mrs. King, that he did *not* commit suicide?" The coroner sounded positively unhappy.

"I don't know what to think." Her distress was beginning to show through. "I suppose anyone's capable of such a thing, at some crisis in life . . . I just don't know."

"Thank you, Mrs. King," young Cabot said hastily at the coroner's surreptitious nod. "You may step down."

Nancy was the last witness.

The coroner gave his formal instructions to the jury, and they filed out to consider their verdict.

Their deliberations lasted six minutes. They brought in a verdict of suicide.

When Layton returned to the courtroom from phoning the *Bulletin,* he had to step aside to allow Hubert Stander and Lola Arkwright to pass. Hathaway was just behind them. Neither Stander nor the red-haired girl so much as glanced his way. But George Hathaway muttered, "Thank you, thank you, Layton," as he went by.

Nancy was still seated in the witness section, her eyes closed. They opened at Layton's step.

"Don't disillusion me, let me dream," Layton said lightly. "You were waiting for me."

"As a matter of fact, yes." She sounded very tired. "Did you drop your car off this morning to be fixed?"

"I did."

"I'll drive you wherever you say. It's the least I can do for all the chauffeuring you've done for me."

"You bet it is! I'd like to have a word with Trimble first, though. Mind waiting a few minutes, Nancy?"

She smiled the faintest, most pathetic smile. "Of course not, Jim. I've spent my life waiting . . . it seems."

Layton said gruffly, "Well, that's all over!" and strode over to the table where Arthur Cabot was still sitting, talking to Sergeant Trimble.

"Thanks for keeping my promise to Hathaway," Layton said to the scarred detective.

Trimble grunted. "What the hell! He's got troubles enough with that bitch who's suing him for divorce."

"You weren't as considerate of Stander."

"Stander," Trimble said, "I don't like."

"You had your hooks into him over that ice pick. What happened?"

The detective grinned wryly. "He's got a lawyer who ought to be in my job, that's what happened. I sure got chewed out."

"What do you mean?"

"We take Stander downtown and this legal eagle hears what we've got. He says, 'Let's go back to Mr. Stander's house.' We go back, and he asks Mrs. Stander one question —what did she do with the ice pick? You know, he hit it on the head? She hefted that behind of hers up to her bedroom, opened a drawer of her vanity, and there it was. She'd borrowed it from the tool drawer in the kitchen to punch a hole in a belt—a new hole, naturally!—and didn't bother to put it back. Bam."

Layton shook his head. With the Stander ice pick found, there was no legal evidence against him sufficient to warrant an indictment. No wonder they had rushed through the inquest.

"At that, you went easy on him," Layton said. "You didn't even mention his shacking up with the redhead."

"Give the old devil his due," the sergeant said dryly. "I had a long session with both of them. Stander wouldn't have swatted a fly because of her. He has a yen for her, sure. But murder?" Trimble shook his head.

"You're convinced, Mr. Cabot, you got a proper verdict?"

The assistant district attorney said stiffly, "If we hadn't been, we wouldn't have settled for it." He seemed to feel the need to add, "To press a murder charge, a D.A. has to have evidence to bring into court. You know that, Layton. In this case, legally speaking, there just isn't any. So what difference does it make?"

"There are thousands of murderers walking around without a care in the world," the glass-eyed detective said with a shrug, "for the same reason. So long, Layton."

"So long," Layton said.

They were right. Society put a premium not on guilt but on proof. Trimble, Cabot, the coroner, the D.A.—they could only obey the rules. Tutter King had been murdered, but for practical purposes he might just as well have committed suicide. The decision of the coroner's jury was merely an exercise in reality.

That's exactly what's wrong with it, Layton thought. Not legally wrong, but *wrong*.

But then Layton was an honest man.

Nancy had managed to find a parking place near the Hall of Justice.

"This was Tutter's," she said, stopping at a sleek white Jaguar. "I usually drive the station wagon, but I always have trouble parking it downtown—I'm an awful driver. Maybe you oughtn't to trust yourself with me. Or would you like to drive?"

The thought of touching the wheel that had been grasped so many times by Tutter King's hands was unpleasant. "I'll take a chance," Layton said. "How about some lunch? I could eat a horse, hoofs and all."

He liked the way she promptly said, "All right, Jim," and slipped behind the wheel, indifferent to who might be watching. It had been different last night! Layton went around the Jaguar and got in beside her. "Where do we go?" she asked.

"Ling's. Ever been there?"

"No."

"It's only a few blocks from here, in old Chinatown."

They were sitting in one of the candlelit booths, protected by beaded curtains and sipping the pungent Chinese tea, when Nancy suddenly said, "I like this, Jim. It's restful . . . intimate."

"That's why I suggested it," Layton said.

Her lashes drooped. "Jim," she said. "Not today. Not now."

So she knew. Layton's heart began to hammer away.

They ate in silence. When Nancy set her fork down with a little sigh of repletion, he lit two cigarettes and put one between her lips and the other between his.

"What did you think of the verdict, Nancy?"

"I don't want to think about it," she said slowly. "The nightmare is over, that's all." Then she smiled and tapped her cigarette ashes into the ash tray. "You've been so good for me, Jim. I don't know how I'd have gone through all this without you."

He knew she meant it, and he knew she had not intended

109

it as an opening. "Made any decisions yet? Like where you're going to live, and so on?"

"I'll stay where I am for a while, anyway. Eventually, I suppose, I'll sell the house and take an apartment in town."

Layton picked up his teacup. "Any idea yet how Tutter was fixed? I mean, how he left you?"

"Tutter's lawyer says I don't have anything to worry about. I won't know the details of the will till after the funeral." She tamped out her cigarette. "I think, Jim, I'd like to go."

"Sure."

She drove him to Joe's. The new windshield had been installed.

"We picked it up secondhand for forty bucks," Joe said. "Plus twelve-fifty for labor, and I put in new wiper blades. This be a charge, Mr. Layton?"

"Who carries all that cash?" Layton grinned. "Thanks, Joe."

"I still think you're nuts," Joe said.

When he had walked back to the Jaguar Layton said, "The buggy's all set, Nancy. You're a doll to have waited."

"Will you be at the funeral?"

"My editor told me to cover it. Sort of a wrap-up."

Nancy King bit her lip. He had to force himself to look away. What a rotten thing to have said to her, he thought. And he thought, Those lips of hers.

"I'm sorry, Nancy. I don't want the assignment. I want to forget Tutter King. I want to forget you were ever Tutter King's wife. I want . . ." It poured out in spite of him.

"Jim, Jim," she said, in a kind of pain. For a moment he caught a glimpse of the old fear in her eyes, the fear he had seen the instant he spotted her in King's studio. "I know what you want. I know." Her gloved hand on his felt like a branding iron.

"And what do you want?" Layton asked roughly.

"I can't . . . I mustn't . . . tell you."

"You've told me!" Great joy flooded him. "Nancy, let me come with you. I want to touch you, hold you, spend all night just looking at you—"

She threw him a wild, tender, confused smile and stepped on the gas. But she had to stop for some passing traffic before she could pull out into the street, and he stood there like a yokel, the carbon of the charge slip fluttering unnoticed from his fingers, gaping at her profile. That exquisite profile. Caught in a cameo moment . . .

Cameos yet.

110

Layton came to himself.

There was no way out.

He was finally, irrevocably, painfully, ecstatically in love.

« 17 »

Layton loved-hated every second of it.

The usual hundreds of rubbernecks surrounded the funeral home. Most of them were teenagers. The police had stretched ropes along each side of the walk from the curb to the entrance and they were busy pressing the crowds back. Put an emcee here with a hand mike and a faceful of teeth, Layton thought, plus a couple of those blockbuster searchlights, and it might just as well be a Hollywood premiere or a supermarket opening.

The mortician's assistants and the police were doing the usual quiet, efficient Los Angeles job of screening would-be gate crashers and giving them the usual quiet, efficient bum's rush. As Layton came up, a dilapidated blonde with blood in her eye was being escorted by a police officer from the inviting open walk into the jam behind the ropes.

"But I tell you Mrs. King is a close personal friend!" the woman was yelling.

"Sure, lady, sure, that's why you don't know her address." The officer grabbed Layton with his free hand. "Hey, bud, where do you think you're going?"

Layton showed his press card. The officer let go, and Layton trudged up the walk and had to produce his card again, and finally he achieved the sanctuary.

An usher with a trained voice—ten to one he's on the books of Central Casting, Layton thought—directed him to the main chapel. "The left two front rows are reserved for the press," the usher said in soft, reverent tones.

"Lucky press," Layton said. The man looked at him, startled. Layton shrugged and stepped into the chapel. It had a capacity of over two hundred, but large patches of empty seats told him that in Hollywood's view the Tutter King funeral was a bright area. King had died under a cloud. The Hollywood that counted disliked clouds. And the great majority of King's friends—the only friends he had apparently had—who could have filled a hundred chapels twice the size, were not being allowed in.

Layton looked through the occupied seats for Nancy. He saw Hubert Stander and, surprisingly, Mrs. Stander; he saw

George Hathaway; he saw young Wayne Mission and Nora Perkins, presumably privileged because of their fan-club status; he saw Hazel Grant, dabbing at her eyes (but she had had a new rinse for the occasion, merrily blue as the sky); he saw a few of the KZZX technical staff, and a morose-looking man in rumpled clothing he recognized as the top-flight press agent who had handled Tutter King's account; but Lola Arkwright was not there, and of Nancy there was no sign.

Of course, he thought. They've put her in the "family" room, for privacy. She won't come in until just before the service starts.

The temptation to join her became so strong that an ache developed in his groin. To discipline himself he walked down to the front of the chapel and deliberately stopped before the casket.

It was set in a forest of flowers. The headpiece had been removed, and Tutter King was looking at the ceiling.

It was queer to think of a corpse looking at a ceiling when the lids had been forcibly shuttered over the eyes. But it was really no queerer than those ancient Roman statues with blanks where the eyes should be—blanks that looked at you quite as convincingly as the real thing.

It was even queer to think of Tutter King in relation to this waxworks figure in the bronze casket. This was the Tussaud dummy in the mould of a man that Nancy had fondled and warmed and been fondled and warmed by for ten years. This thing, when it had blood in its veins instead of embalming fluid, stuck an ice pick into its living heart. Saith the state of California. Saith Jim Layton of the Los Angeles *Bulletin:* This thing was foully done in by a grand larcenist of its breath and being who's getting away with it.

And I'm inheriting its wife.

And I'm glad. Jim Layton, the last honest man, is so damn full of gladness it's become a hurt in the groin.

Layton started at a tap on his shoulder.

"Looks pretty good, doesn't he?" said the dry *sotto* of Sergeant Harry Trimble.

"Hello, Sergeant."

"Well, that's what you're supposed to say over the bum that's been degutted and laid out, isn't it?"

"What are you doing here?"

"Oh, I'm kind of at loose ends. I don't like loose ends, Layton."

"Neither do I."

They stared down at what was left of Tutter King.

"This one's going to haunt me till I'm lying where he is," the one-eyed detective muttered. "Ah, let's sit down."

112

Layton slipped into the aisle seat in the row immediately behind the press section. His colleagues gave him a unified glare, then turned back to their chores.

The sergeant sat down beside him.

The hell with them, Layton thought. The hell with you, too, he said silently to the detective at his side. I know what I want and I've got it . . . He grinned deeply inside. He could imagine what the boys of news town would be saying when Lonesome Jim Layton took unto his bosom the midnight-haired widow of Tutter King.

And then he saw her.

He saw her, and his heart was in his throat in a wild leap, and he wanted to go to her so badly that he began to itch all over.

She was coming in slowly with two elderly couples, ushered to the front of the chapel, near the casket, by the mortuary's head man himself. Special wing chairs were waiting for them, so that when they sat down the public view of them was largely cut off and they could indulge their grief in a variable percentage of privacy, depending on where the lesser mourners were seated.

His glimpse of her was a flick and an eternity.

Layton sat back, satisfied.

This is your day, Tutter, he thought.

Tomorrow is mine.

Layton paid no attention to the service. It was in the little white hands of a clergyman whose resonant response to the proximity of the dead man was in no way impaired by the fact that they had never met in life. He delivered the customary fervid eulogy, investing the dear departed with all but visible wings.

Layton could see the merest segment of Nancy, a long, narrow plinth, but he was in a mood to exult over even a bit of her. The sliver of cheek in view seemed no paler than it usually was. The single sable eyelash was lowered. She was in unostentatious black and she wore no mourning veil.

The elderly people between whom she was sitting were her parents, he guessed. She had told him once—how long ago it seemed!—that her folks live in Oregon; her father was a country doctor. He was a worn, fragile-looking man and his hand, like a dried insect, lay quietly on hers. Her mother seemed a cipher, a small, sweet nonentity, too naïve to pretend distress over a man she had not known. Nancy looked like her father.

The other elderly couple were evidently Tutter King's father and mother. Layton looked away.

I love you, he said to the sliver of pale cheek, I love you.

113

It amused him that he felt no quiver of shame at repeating in the privacy of his head the oldest cliché known to man. I love you, Nancy . . .

When it was all over, Layton caught the arm of a columnist for the *Bulletin* who was covering the funeral from the woman's angle and said, "You going out to Forest Lawn, Cissie?"

"Well, sure."

"Do me a favor and cover for me, will you?"

"Why, where are you going?" the woman asked suspiciously.

"Oh, nuts, Cis, I can't take any more of this. Be nice, huh? I'll scratch your back some time."

"That'll be the day," she sniffed. "I've been trying to arouse the spark of manhood in you for years."

"You're just not my type." Layton grinned.

"Who is—King's widow?"

He pretended amused indignation. "Come again?"

"I heard you had a thing for her."

"Can you beat that," Layton said, shaking his head. "So now I'm a casket robber."

The newspaperwoman kept watching him. "She's a pretty little thing."

"So's my grandmother." Layton gave her a friendly shove. "Go on, Cissie, before they leave you at the rail. And thanks. Remind me to buy you a drink."

He could feel her scalpel glance probing his back as he made for the phone booths. The hell with her, too. She'd have plenty to yack about soon enough.

By the time he was through phoning in his report of the service, the cortege of glittering black Cadillacs had departed for the cemetery. Layton strolled out of the funeral home, stifling an impulse to whistle. The bulk of the mob had dispersed; the police were coiling the ropes. To his surprise, Wayne Mission and Nora Perkins were standing disconsolately on the sidewalk.

"Hi, kids," Layton said, looking from one to the other.

"Oh, hello, Mr. Layton." Young Mission's tone was glum. The girl's plump cheeks were smeary and her marbly little eyes were swollen from weeping. "Aren't you going to Forest Lawn, either?"

"I'm not high on cemeteries, Wayne. But how come you two didn't go?"

"We forgot to ask in advance. They didn't assign us to a car, and I couldn't get my father's heap for today."

"Who cares?" Nora Perkins said sullenly. "I'm sorry I even came for the service."

"That's great, that's a fine thing to say," Wayne snapped.

114

"It would look nice, wouldn't it, if the president and vice president of Tutter King's original fan club didn't show up for his funeral! Sometimes I don't dig you at all, Nora."

"So you don't! Anyway, I'm going home."

"Don't you think you'd better go back to school?" Layton asked.

"Oh, we got excused for today," the boy muttered. "Well—see you, Mr. Layton."

"Wait a minute," Layton said. "Where do you two live?"

"I'm on Asbury, twenty-nine hundred block. Nora's on Elm. They're out in the Highland Park district, off San Fernando Road."

"I'll drive you home."

"You don't have to do that, Mr Layton," the girl said with a trace of interest. "We'll take the bus."

"Come on, both of you."

"Gosh, Mr. Layton, this is awfully nice of you . . ."

The niceness was in the kids, Layton thought as he headed for the downtown Freeway interchange. The professional mourners could wring their hands over juvenile degeneration in the atomic age, but the fact was that kids like these displayed sturdier qualities of character and worth than the clay-footed idols they worshiped. They knew faith and they practiced loyalty. It was the so-called grown-up world that broke them down and embittered enough of them to create a social problem.

"What did you think of the funeral?" Layton said.

"It was horrible." Nora shivered. "I don't ever want to go to one again."

"That minister saying all those things about Tutter," Wayne said. "How would he know? He didn't know Tutter."

Neither did you, Layton said, but not aloud. And maybe that's just as well.

He was turning into the Pasadena Freeway when Wayne Mission said suddenly, "People are rats. Where were all the big shots Tutter knew from show business? His friends—stars!" The boy snorted. "They're crums, that's all they are. Rats jumping off the sinking ship. . . . I don't care what anybody says. Tutter was real cool. He was sure nice to Nora and me."

"Maybe he was, and maybe he wasn't," the girl said in a tight voice.

The goggled boy shook his head. "How do you like that! Nora's sore, Mr. Layton, because Tutter was married. So what? It didn't make any difference to me."

"It wouldn't," the girl retorted. "You're not a woman."

"Well, neither are you!"

115

Nora sank back, furious but silenced.

After a while young Mission stirred. "That inquest yesterday, Mr. Layton."

"What about it?"

"Why was all that stuff brought up about murder?"

"Because," Layton said, gently and carefully, "some people thought it might have been. The way Tutter died . . . people don't often commit suicide that way."

"Yeah," the boy said thoughtfully, "that bothered me, too. But who'd want to kill a wonderful person like Tutter? So it must have been suicide, the way the jury said."

"He shouldn't have done it, he shouldn't!" Nora said passionately. "He had so much to live for."

"Wait a minute, Nora! Mr. Layton, what did you think?"

"Look, can't we talk about something else?" Layton said lightly. "The verdict is in, Tutter's dead and being buried—"

"No, I mean it, Mr. Layton," Wayne Mission said. "I've been giving this a lot of thought, and it doesn't add up, somehow. Did you think it was murder?"

Layton sighed. "Well, there were some possible motives. And, of course, a number of people had the opportunity—"

"That's one of the things been bugging me. I read all the testimony, and I don't see this opportunity stuff at all. The news-break intermission was only ten minutes all told, and some of that was taken up by Tutter's leaving Studio A and going to his dressing room—of course, it's only a few steps, but even a few steps take time—and then having to cross the hall to dressing room 1 and all . . . What I mean, except for Mr. Stander I myself didn't see a soul, and I was out there in the hall must have been a good four minutes."

"You were in the hall four minutes?" Layton asked. "You must be mistaken, Wayne."

"No," Wayne protested.

"But you told Sergeant Trimble that you and Nora went to Tutter's dressing room, looked in, he wasn't there, and then you returned to the studio. That couldn't have taken four minutes."

"Well, of course, not *that* part of it," the boy said. "What took up most of the time was I had to wait for Nora." He glanced philosophically at the girl, who glared back at him. "You know girls when they have to go to the john. It's a wonder I'm not standing there yet."

"Wayne Mission," the girl hissed, her face flaming, "you're *impossible!* Isn't anything sacred?"

"Well, I had to explain, didn't I?"

"Just a moment," Layton said. "Which john are you talking about, Wayne?"

"The ladies' room right outside Studio A. You know, Mr. Layton. It's the only one in that corridor."

"I don't know *why* we have to discuss things like *that*," Nora Perkins said. "I'm sure there must be more acceptable subjects for conversation."

"No, wait, Nora," Layton said. "Why didn't you mention this to Sergeant Trimble?"

"That I had to visit the ladies' room?" The girl eyed him coldly.

"It's all my fault." Wayne said disgustedly. "I shouldn't have brought it up. I'll never hear the end of it."

"You certainly won't!"

"But that might have been important, Nora," Layton said.

"Oh, for heaven's sake," the girl said petulantly. "It was no such thing, Mr. Layton. The only person either Wayne or I laid eyes on from the time we left Studio A until we went back in was that Mr. Stander down at the end of the hall, going to the control room of Studio B and C. And we told the detective that. *Now* can we talk about something else?"

« 18 »

Layton dropped the two teenagers at their homes, drove off carefully, and stopped carefully at the first tavern he saw.

He carefully downed four shots of bourbon, neat, in rapid succession, sat musing for a while, then ordered two more.

When he returned to his car he drove, still more carefully, to the Freeway. He took the slow lane because his head felt large, light, and tippy.

He parked downtown and began shuffling through the streets, hands plunged in his trouser pockets and his shoulders up near his ears, as if he were cold.

An hour or so later he went into another bar.

He reached his apartment at a quarter to four the next morning, long after the official closing time of Los Angeles bistros. He reached it on his hands and knees. He had little recollection of events past midnight. He had been rolled somewhere, and survival instinct had kept him from attempting to drive home. There was the vaguest memory of a cab-driver to whom he had given his wrist watch in payment for depositing him at his door. That had been ages before, because he had had to creep across the sidewalk and into the building and up the stairs, a time-consuming procedure.

Now he found himself safely ensconced in his nest, surrounded by a horrible odor. Something died in here, he said to himself with great amusement, and I guess it's you. You stink, old boy, all over. Inside as well as out.

He forced his eyes to stay open by pure cussedness and took a floor's-eye view of himself. It was pitiful. He felt so sad at what he saw that he began to cry.

He stopped crying long enough to be sick again, this time over his own floor, and then he cried some more.

The next thing he knew, he was dialing the *Bulletin*. Or trying to. He tried six times, but each time something went wrong. Finally he dialed the operator and made a desperate effort.

"Look, sweetheart, I can't seem to get my number, wouzhyou get it for me?" He articulated the number. "Liferdeath."

He heard a ladylike sniff and then after a while Layton woke up with a voice saying in his ear, "Come on! Who is this?"

"Watshon?" That was funny. He didn't remember asking for the night desk. "Wonnerful age the age velectronics, Watshon."

"Say," the voice said, "This couldn't be Jim Layton, could it?"

"Well, whonell dyathink it izh?"

"Where are you, Jim?"

"Home," Layton said indignantly.

"Then you must have just got there. Dracula's out for your blood, Jimmie boy. Where've you been all day?"

"Watshon, lish . . . shen." Layton swallowed. "Listen. Msick. Mdamsick. Can't come ininamorning. Tella Cheese."

"You may never have to come in," Watson said. "Not if I read the signs and portents correctly. What's happened, Jim? I've never known you to be drunk before."

"Whosh drunk?" Layton wept.

"Jim"—Watson sounded concerned now—"how about my sending one of the boys over? You sound like you need help."

Layton said, spacing it out, "Not—'like you need'—Watshon. *A zif.*"

"You're okay." Watson laughed. "Go to bed, Jim." He hung up.

When Layton opened his eyes his first thought was that

118

the Russians had dropped the big one and his whole apartment had been picked up by the scruff of its neck, shaken, and dropped back helter-skelter. The telephone table was lying on its top like an overturned turtle, the phone was off its cradle and buzzing feebly for help, some animal had left a mess on the rug, the couch was in the wrong place, a picture had been knocked off the wall and its glass shattered, and there was a zigzag trail of crumpled, smeared, noisome clothing leading from the mess on the rug to the fallen telephone and back across the room to the bathroom. At this point Layton closed his eyes. The one glimpse he had had of his bathroom was just too, too much.

When he opened his eyes again he crawled off the divan and began the work of rehabilitation. He was not surprised to find himself naked, although he never slept naked; rather, he was grateful. The vision of himself falling asleep in the befouled wreckage of his clothing was too sickening to contemplate for more than a moment.

It was not until he was scalding his hide under the shower, with the apartment reasonably restored and most of the stench gone, that he remembered. The shock that followed the memory struck him with concussive force. In one soundless stroke it crushed out his hangover, vaporized the mush on his brain . . . cleansed him to the bone so that he cowered, inwardly naked as well, before the unveiled granite face of truth.

Layton emptied a six-cup pot of coffee. Three cups he drank black, the rest he took with cream and sugar. He made no toast. Although he had not swallowed a morsel of solid food for almost twenty-four hours, the mere thought churned his stomach.

He had to retrace his erratic route of the night before to reclaim his car.

It was almost 3 P.M. when he swung into the driveway. The doors of the double garage were open. The white Jaguar was there, the station wagon was not.

Nevertheless, Layton thumbed the doorbell. He thumbed it several times without result.

He returned to his car, backed out of the driveway, and parked on the street. Then he trudged over to the swimming pool, lowered himself into an aluminum-slatted chair, and waited.

At a quarter to four the station wagon pulled into the driveway. Seeing him, Nancy waved and drove on into the garage. He was at the front door when she came out of the garage.

"Hello, Jim." She did not seem surprised to see him. "Waiting long?"

"Not long."

"I had to drive my father and mother to the airport. Poor dears, they're all worn out. I wanted them to stay a few days, but dad had to get back to his practice. Did I ever tell you my dad is a doctor?"

"Yes," Layton said.

"I'm sorry you didn't meet them, Jim." She unlocked the door and went in, and he followed her. "I think you'd have liked one another."

Layton shut the door, bolted it, and put the guard chain in place. Nancy had stopped at the little wall mirror in the foyer to take off her hat and remove her gloves and give her incredible mass of jet hair a few pokes. At the sound of the bolt and guard chain she turned in surprise.

"I hope you're not expecting anybody," Layton said.

"No." She frowned ever so little. "What's the matter, Jim? Is something wrong?" Her tone lightened. "Lose your job, or fall in love?"

Layton stood there looking at her. He was not conscious of any emotion at all. It was as if the thalamic function that made it possible for him to feel pain had stopped working, starting a paralytic process that had reached to the tiniest ganglia of his nervous system.

"I'm sorry, Jim," Nancy said quietly. "I know now there's something dreadfully the matter. Let's go into the living room."

He followed her in.

"Sit down."

He remained standing.

She glanced at him in a puzzled rather than an apprehensive way. "Will you have a drink?"

"Yesterday was for drinking," Layton said. "Today is for being cold, dead sober."

"Was it the funeral, Jim? I . . . looked for you at the cemetery, but I didn't see you, although I did catch a glimpse of you in the chapel before the service."

She came to him and touched his hand. "I know, Jim, I know you've fallen in love with me. I . . . feel a great deal for you, too. So soon . . . It's confused me. I mean . . . I want you to put your arms around me, Jim, oh, I do. I want you to kiss me, and I want to kiss you. But . . . not yet."

"Please don't do that," Layton said, staring down at her hand.

"I'm sorry," she murmured. "That was stupidly, thoughtlessly female. I'm sorry, Jim." She went over to the big

120

chair near the fireplace and sat down, tucking one leg under her like a little girl. "I realize how hard it must have been for you yesterday, having to come to my husband's funeral, having to watch me in the role of his widow—"

"If I'd known then what I know now," Layton said, "I might have enjoyed your performance."

"What do you mean, Jim?" Her hands groped for the chair arms and clutched.

Layton went over to the fireplace and put his forearm on the mantelpiece and rested his head on his forearm. Her eyes followed him, hugely troubled.

"I can't remember the time when the very thought of doing a dishonest thing didn't shame and frighten me, Nancy. It's been very easy for me to be honest, considering the way I was brought up. When I was old enough to analyze it, it even bothered me. I felt there was something unnatural about me. I asked an acquaintance of mine once, a psychiatrist, whether that wasn't so, as if honesty were abnormal, a disease. He was surprised. He said he didn't remember ever having been asked that question in just that way, and that to attempt to answer it he'd have to take me on as a patient." Layton laughed. "Can you tie that? Be honest, and you need a psychiatrist."

He stopped laughing, and the room was very quiet. "I've often wondered just how honest I really am. It's been a cinch for me to turn down bribes to sit on a story or kill it. I haven't had the least trouble returning lost wallets to their owners intact. It's perfectly simple for me to resist defrauding an insurance company, even though it's the kind of fraud most people indulge in and the companies have given up trying to lick. I've even been honest in the other sense, as far as I know—with myself, I mean. To thine own self be true—that jazz. But you know something? Yesterday I found out I'd never been put to the test. The real test. Where you love somebody, and she loves you—you think —and you've got to make a decision that involves not money, not ethics, but your lives . . . both your lives."

He swung around. The liquid eyes were so full of pain that he had to steel himself to keep from looking away.

Layton walked over to stand before her. She stared up at him, silent and bloodless. "It's even tougher than that, Nancy. Because, you see, I don't have to do anything *actively* dishonest, just keep my mouth shut. The yen to do exactly that is so damn powerful it tore me apart yesterday, and today it's paralyzed me." But the mechanism of pain—was it turned on by hers?—began working again without warning. Layton groped to a nearby chair. He sat down with a groan.

121

"Jim." It was the faintest echo of a whisper.

Her pallor was so deathly as she sat across from him, her eyes so distended, her body so frozen, that Layton jumped up and began walking up and down. Anything—anything to keep from having to look at her.

After a moment he said in a rational voice, "I drove Nora Perkins and Wayne Mission home from the funeral parlor yesterday. You remember—the president and vice president of the Tutter King Los Angeles Fan Club.

"The boy insisted on discussing your husband's death, and in the course of it dropped something neither he nor the girl had mentioned when Trimble questioned them. Wayne said that after he and Nora looked into Tutter's dressing room during the intermission and didn't see him there, Nora stopped in the ladies' room before they went back to Studio A. The kid said that, all told, he must have been waiting in the corridor there some four minutes, most of it while Nora was in the john. As far as he was concerned, the only human being he laid eyes on during the whole time was Stander, down at the end of the hall, headed for the Studio B and C control room."

"I don't . . . understand." She sounded so helplessly tired that Layton found himself grinding his teeth.

"Don't you, Nancy? I'll refresh your memory. We'll start from the time Tutter left Studio A, at the news break. He was immediately followed by Lola Arkwright, and just then Hathaway left his office. King stopped for a moment to let Lola catch up with him, and Hathaway was practically on their heels. Tutter went into his dressing room, Lola walked on a few steps and went into hers—next door—and Hathaway continued down the hall to the B-C control booth."

It was like something out of a dream, or a movie, or anything make-believe—his walking about calmly reciting what they both knew, as if any of it were necessary. Yet he went on, driven by a compulsion to be logical, to wrap it up . . . that was it, to wrap it up, get rid of it. Out of his system? But then what?

"Then you came out of Studio A, Nancy. You told Trimble you walked up to Tutter's dressing room, saw the door was shut, decided not to go in after all, went into the ladies' room next door to the studio, and from the ladies' room returned to the studio.

"I was about twenty seconds or more later than you leaving Studio A. By the time I got into the hall you would have had to be in the ladies' room to account for my not seeing you, if your story was the truth.

"I walked down the corridor looking into dressing rooms with their doors open, then I walked back. I'd certainly have heard the door of the ladies' room open while my back was turned; I noticed when I first got to the station that its automatic closing gadget is out of order, and the noise the door makes being opened and closed by hand in those halls is loud and startling. And when I was coming back up the hall I'd certainly have seen as well as heard you coming out. So when I turned into the other arm of the L, you must still—according to your story—have been in the ladies' room.

"Hathaway's office door is only a few steps from where the corridors meet and the Studio A and ladies' room doors are situated. Stander came out of Hathaway's office as I approached to go in. I went into the office; Stander walked on. He turned into the arm of the L I'd just come from and proceeded toward the B-C control booth. And what did Stander say? That after noticing me go into Hathaway's office he saw and heard *no* one until he got down toward the end of the hall. That, Nancy, still leaves you in the ladies' room.

"As Stander got to the far end of the hall Wayne Mission and Nora Perkins stepped out of Studio A. Remember, you're still in the ladies' room. The kids looked into Tutter's dressing room, found it empty, turned back . . . *and Wayne waited in the hall while Nora went into the ladies' room.*"

She was leaning back in the chair now in an exhausted way, her head uptilted, watching his lips.

"This is what Nora Perkins told me yesterday, Nancy. I can quote her exact words; there are some things that burn into your brain like acid." And now Layton's eyes were burning. "She said: 'The only person either Wayne *or I* laid eyes on from the time we left Studio A until we went back in was that Mr. Stander down at the end of the hall.' I ask you: Since the recap I've just gone through places you in that ladies' room when Nora went in, why didn't she see you? *Because, Nancy, you weren't there.*"

Layton leaned over her. She did not react in any way.

"I didn't believe it at first. I tried to give you an out, find one for you. But I couldn't. If it had been the usual public ladies' room you might have been in one of the stalls, and conceivably Nora might not have noticed you. But it isn't the usual public ladies' room, Nancy. It's like a small private bathroom; all it has is a washbowl and an open toilet —not even a window. As a matter of fact, had you been in that ladies' room, Nancy, *Nora couldn't have got in at all.* It bolts from inside, and you'd hardly have gone in without bolting it.

"But just to make absolutely sure I asked Nora: Was
123

anyone in there when she went in? Of course she said no. In fact, what she said was: 'How could there have been?'

"I wriggled, and I squirmed, and I fought and bled to get you out of that damn ladies' room in a reasonable, legitimate way. But in the end it all came down to the same thing: Your story, combined with the others' stories, placed you in the ladies' room; and you weren't.

"So, Nancy, you lied to Trimble. You hadn't gone into the ladies' room in the first place. Why would you lie about a trivial thing like that? Here's the answer I've had to come up with, Nancy—look at me!" He seized her chin and forced her head up. "The answer is: *You lied because you were with Tutter in dressing room 1, sticking an ice pick into his heart.* Now tell me where I'm wrong. Tell me!"

He felt a froth form at the corner of his mouth and, as if awakening from a nightmare, he released her chin and licked the froth away and straightened up.

But Nancy's head drooped and she shut her eyes.

"Tell me, Nancy," Layton pleaded quietly. "For God's sake, tell me."

Nancy got up. She walked out into the foyer and picked up her bag and came back, opening it, searching for a cigarette, a lighter.

"No, Jim," she said at his automatic movement. "You just sit down."

He sat down. She found the cigarette and the lighter and she sat down opposite him with the bag in her lap and inhaled deeply.

"The Arkwright woman doesn't know it," she said, "but she missed out by a hair. Before Tutter left for the station Friday he told me that he'd done a lot of thinking since KZZX canceled his contract. He told me that since his disc-jockey career was over and he had to build a new career for himself, he'd decided to make a clean sweep. He wanted a divorce."

She leaned back, smoking hungrily.

"He wanted a divorce from me, and he was going to marry Lola Arkwright. He smiled at me and said, yes, he knew she was a tramp, but she was wonderful in bed—something I, apparently, had never been for him. They were *muy simpático* as lovers, and Lola was so desperate for respectability that she'd stop being a tramp the moment he put a wedding ring on her finger. Do you know something, Jim? I wouldn't be surprised if he was right about her. Tutter was very shrewd when it came to sizing up women. The reason Lola was so confused is that his entire career, based as it was on the admiration of women, had made him supercautious in his relations with them, as well

124

as contemptuous. It was characteristic that Tutter would give his wife the bounce without committing himself in so many words to her successor. Actually he told me he was going to announce his engagement to Lola at the end of the telecast. That was to be his big surprise—to her, I suppose. She'd had to guess at it. He'd been so vague with her that she was able to talk herself out of it afterward. I think the whole idea of announcing his engagement on the air as his sign-off was motivated by his basic contempt for women. Down deep Tutter hated the millions of women, from adolescents to grandmothers, who drooled every time he opened his mouth. It was his way of expressing his hatred."

Layton nodded slowly. "Tell me, Nancy. How come everything Trimble turned up about your private life indicated that you and King were happily married?"

"Why shouldn't it? I thought so, too." Nancy flipped her cigarette into the fireplace. Her eyes had cleared, her voice was strong and steady now. "I wonder if you can imagine, Jim, what happened to me when—out of a clear sky, without the slightest warning—Tutter pronounced my fate. I'd known about Lola, and there'd been other women, and he knew I knew—but I'd let him, or myself, talk me into believing they were meaningless. Of course, I was a fool. I really loved him. For ten years I'd kept myself buried, like a mole, watching the man I loved besieged by armies of other women, sleeping with some of them . . . kept myself buried willingly, because I thought I was the only woman really important in his life, and that by keeping myself buried I was furthering my loved and loving husband's career.

"And he blew it all up in my face with one word on Friday morning.

"What happened to me, Jim," Nancy went on, steadily still, "was that after he left the house I went into the kitchen and rummaged around in a drawer and found an ice pick that had been lying there unused for years, and I put it in my bag and drove down to KZZX. I could have used the gun he'd bought me years ago—for protection, he said, when I was here alone—but I saw no reason to shoot him and be caught because of the noise and have to throw away the rest of my life with his . . . Look at me, Jim. Look at me."

And now it was his turn to force his glance.

"It was premeditated murder. I knew just what I was going to do. I went there armed with a silent weapon, intending to kill him and get away with it. I knew all about his intermissions, his routine. I lied when I said I went to dressing room 2 and decided not to go in. I did go in, and Tutter was there alone. The moment he saw me he suggest-

125

ed going across the hall. I knew why. Lola Arkwright was in the next dressing room, and he thought I was going to make a scene, and Lola would overhear and find out he'd been living with me all the years he'd told her he was having nothing to do with me. He took me by the arm and ran me across the hall to that unoccupied dressing room, and he shut the door with great care, so that no one would hear us. He did it so fast we were in dressing room 1 before you had time, apparently, to step out of Studio A."

"And you waited till Tutter turned around, and you took the ice pick out of your bag, and you let him have it—face to face." It came out in a croak, and he cleared his throat.

Nancy nodded. "Face to face, Jim. I wanted him to know that he couldn't throw a woman's life away as if she were an old hat—not without paying for it, and I don't mean money. I told the truth about not knowing anything about his finances. I still don't, beyond what his lawyer told me over the weekend . . . No, Jim, let me finish.

"I'd wiped the handle clean before I left home. After that I kept my gloves on. When he was lying on the floor I wrapped his hand around the ice pick in the normal way. It . . . wouldn't keep holding on." For the first time her voice faltered; but it was only for a moment. "I did want it to look like suicide, Jim. I saw no reason why I—or anyone else, for that matter—should have to pay for his worthless life."

"When did you go back to the studio?" he muttered.

"It must have been just seconds before you did; I'd purposely waited in room 1 till the ten minutes of the intermission were almost over. I was lucky, wasn't I? Nobody saw me, coming or going, in all that corridor traffic." She smiled. "And neither of us would be in this position today if that girl fan of Tutter's hadn't had to go to the toilet. Which reminds me. Does your honesty extend to expressing your real intentions when most people say, 'Excuse me, I have to go wash my hands'?" She rose from the chair and came to him, and, very lightly, pressed her lips to his forehead. "Excuse me, Jim, I have to go wash my hands."

Before he could touch her, or rise, she was going quickly to her bedroom. She turned in the bedroom doorway to smile at him, and then she went in and closed the door.

Layton sat limply, like an old man. What was he to do now?

I can say nothing, nothing at all, about this, he thought. To anyone. Neither Nora nor Wayne had the faintest suspicion of the significance of the girl's revelation of yesterday.

The case is closed. It's suicide. The coroner's jury said so. Closed. And he's buried.

126

And then I get to marry the girl, not quite as in the movies. Because I want her, I have need of her, I have need of her love and of mine. And would we live happily ever after...?

He tried to clear his head, shaking it as if there were water in his ears. Happily ever after . . . Me? Knowing I had, by an act of dishonest omission, sanctioned the taking of a human life . . . ? knowing that the hand I kissed, the hand that caressed me, even though with truest tenderness and deepest love, had plunged a steel blade into a living heart?

Maybe if they knew—maybe if she were tried and at her trial the people on the jury were made to understand what had driven her to murder . . . Layton shook his head. It was, as she said, cold-blooded, premeditated murder. She didn't have a chance.

And she knew it.

"And I know it," Layton said aloud, startling himself. And I know it, he said in silence.

Yet how can I turn her in? How can mine be the voice that sends the message of her guilt and pronounces the sentence of her doom over the lines strung between Chapter Drive and downtown Los Angeles? What, after all, has she done to have to die for it—at *my* hand?

She's committed murder.

What price honesty now?

Layton you honest man, you. Is your honesty so damn precious to you . . . ?

Almost he came to a decision.

Almost.

But, trembling on the brink, he heard a sound.

It was the report of a gun, and it came from beyond the bedroom door.

Layton found her on the bed. She had placed the muzzle of a pistol in her mouth and squeezed the trigger. What he saw, on the pillow, on the headboard, on the bed itself, made him totter into the bathroom and fall to his knees over the bowl.

It was Sergeant Trimble, a very long time later, who came up to Layton's apartment and walked in without knocking and over to where Layton was lying in the dark staring up at nothing, and who said to Layton: "I found this under the pillow where she shot herself. It's addressed to you, Jim. I have a photostat for the files—it's okay. You keep this."

Layton felt something flutter onto his chest.

After a moment Sergeant Trimble went away.

Layton stirred. He had been lying there for so long that

127

his muscles felt atrophied. He stretched; his joints sounded like rusty door hinges.

His hand went groping to his chest. He found it.

Then he got up from the couch and fumbled around in the dark until he located the light switch.

He sank into a chair, blinking at it.

It was a sheet of notepaper of fine quality but an aged look, as if it had been bought a long time ago. There was an embossed NK in gold in the upper left corner, but she had taken her pen and slashed up and down and across it several times.

The letter said:

Dearest, dearest Jim—There's only one answer to your problem and to mine, and this is it.

It would be too cruel to make you decide. And in the end, even if you decided for me instead of for what you've always believed in, your love would turn to loathing.

I know, Jim. It happened to me.

Please try to explain to my dad and mother, especially my dad. I mean why I did what I did—why I killed Tutter and, much more important, why I killed myself. They won't understand, but please—try, anyway.

I was saying good-by when I kissed you on the forehead just before going into the bedroom. I wanted so much to kiss you the way we've both wanted to, but I knew if I did I wouldn't have the courage to go through with this.

Good-by, Jim darling, good-by.